THE FERA

SPACE MARAUDER CHRONICLES
BOOK ONE

LORENA PARA

For you, dear reader.
May you find the courage
to live your dreams.

Copyright © 2021 by Lorena Para

Second Edition 2024

eBook edition September 2021
Paperback edition September 2021
Paperback and ebook editions revised 2024

Book design by Lorena Para
Cover image by Ronnie Jensen
www.tegnemaskin.no

ISBN 978-1-7375253-0-1 (paperback)
ASIN B09DY2KZ4J (ebook)

Get a free bonus story at
TheShortWriter.com

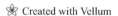 Created with Vellum

CONTENTS

*O*rinthia Anton was running late. Again. It was the same day and time every week, but she never managed to arrive when she was supposed to. She grunted and cursed herself with every step.

Hover cars zoomed overhead, high above the buildings surrounding the city. Early morning vendors called out from their shops and stalls as she ran by. Smells of cooked meats and freshly baked treats barely registered in her mind. A group of children dressed in school uniforms moved to the side to avoid being trampled.

At the end of the crowded street, Orinthia skidded through the entrance of a flower shop. She braced herself on her knees and tried to catch her breath as a jingle from a speaker somewhere in the room announced her entry.

"Late again, I see." An elderly man chuckled from behind the counter.

The smell of fresh cut flowers filled her nostrils as she inhaled deep to gain control of her lungs. "Is there enough time to place my order?" Orinthia asked.

"Already done, my dear." The man hobbled to the cooler

where a dozen flower arrangements waited, suspended behind clear glass. The door hissed as the seal broke, and a tiny cloud drifted out. The mist encircled him, dissipating shortly after the door closed.

"Shue, you're a lifesaver," Orinthia said.

"Anything for my best and most regular customer."

Orinthia closed the distance between the entrance and counter, tapping her watch on the metal card reader to pay. "Payment declined, please try again," a bubbly robotic woman's voice declared.

"Uh," Orinthia said. She bit her bottom lip as she tapped her watch a second time.

"Payment declined, please try again," the voice repeated.

Orinthia's face burned with embarrassment as she mumbled curses to herself. "I must be over-credited again."

"I'll put it in my log," Shue said. "Take the flowers now. I know your mama loves her zinnias. Be sure to pay my daughter, Mansha, when you come in next week. Arna and I are going to visit our eldest son. He and his wife recently moved to the Moon colonies, and it'll be our first time there."

"Promise I will," Orinthia said, taking the bouquet as he handed it to her.

Before Shue could say anything else, Orinthia was out the door and sprinted full speed down the street. Tipping the flowers in her hand, she checked the time on her watch. If she had looked up a moment sooner, she could have avoided running shoulder first into the stone figure in her path.

To save the flowers, she used the force of the impact to toss herself on her side, rolling with them tucked safely in her arms. The young woman lay on the pavement, sore and breathless.

"That was impressive," a man said, as if he had watched

her stick the landing to a backflip rather than colliding into him. He held out his hand. "You 'right?"

Orinthia remained on her back, still clutching the bouquet. Her elbow burned from scraping against the concrete, and the cool breeze on her skin told her she had torn the sleeve of her jacket.

"You'd be surprised how often that actually happens," she said, refusing his aid and pushing herself up.

"Let me at least get that for you," the man said, as he motioned to her bleeding wound. Before she could object, he reached into his coat and pulled out a silver vial. He popped the lid and let two drops of thick blue liquid fall onto her flesh. "That should do it."

The fluid fizzed for a second or two. Almost instantly, the pain subsided, and the blood dried up. Within moments, the wound closed and vanished, along with any trace of injury aside from the ripped fabric.

"Thanks." Orinthia looked up from her arm to properly examine the man standing before her.

The stone man replaced the vial in his coat. His hands were made entirely of crystal from fingertip to forearm. The crystal smoothly fused with the stone peeking from under his cuffed sleeves. She let her eyes wander almost straight upward to see his face. He had no hair on top of his head. But then she thought, *how would stone even grown hair?*

"Where're you headed in such a hurry?" the man asked.

His question brought her back to the present. She looked at her watch again, which was now scratched from the fall. "Shoot!" She did not bother to answer him and ran once again toward the appointment for which she was already ten minutes late.

"You're welcome!" the man shouted as she faded into the distance.

Rounding the corner, she sped through an open iron gate and up the gravel path to the top of the hill where her mother waited.

"Sorry I'm late." Orinthia panted. "These are for you." The paper rustled around the bouquet as she set it on the grass beside a tall stone. She touched the engraving.

Jean Anton. Mother, Wife, Friend.
12-05-2560 / 1-30-2601

ORINTHIA SAT in silence beside her mother's gravestone, overlooking the holographic burial marker below. A breeze echoed the coolness of the morning. The cemetery was still except for a handful of birds jumping and chirping through the branches of trees in the distance. Even the skies were clear, since the airspace above the cemetery was a strict no-fly zone to honor the dead.

Able to finally breathe normally, Orinthia pulled out the PortTab from her coat pocket. "Glad this didn't break. Adora would have killed me if I came back with another broken one."

The facial recognition lit up the screen. "Good morning, Officer Anton." the virtual assistant said. "Reminder. Briefing begins in fifteen minutes. Shall I read the rest of our schedule?"

"No, I'm good. Open journal."

"There are three new entries. Should I read them?"

"Switch to manual." Orinthia pressed a button on the edge of the device, muting the voice. She scrolled through the notes she made over the week. "Uri should be home soon from his tour of the Moon's cyborg hospitals," she spoke to her mother's grave. "I think helping them helps him just as much. They make him feel like he's not alone."

Alone. She swallowed down the emotion tugging at her chest and tucked it away for later where she could revisit it with a strong drink in her hand. "He said he'd come with me to see you next week."

"Oh," she continued. "Remember that guy I arrested a month ago? Well, he's out now. Arsenio said it's because I didn't wait for the warrant before searching his ship. Really? I knew he would be destroying evidence while we stood around. And I was right." Orinthia sighed. "They break rules all the time. I only bend a few to get the job done. Criminals don't follow the law, so why do we have to in order to apprehend them?"

Another breeze blew strands of her silver hair against her cheek. "I won't be like that when I'm a captain. A title won't change me. They just need to give me the promotion."

Her watch vibrated and sounded a whistling alarm. There was so much she wanted to talk about, but her late start also made her late for work.

"I better go. Adoracion said she'll start docking my pay if I'm late again. Hopefully when I come back, I'll be Captain Orinthia." She stood up and touched the top of her mother's gravestone. "Wish me luck."

"**G**ood morning, Officer Anton." A woman's face appeared on the screen beside the door as Orinthia snuck into the Galactic Marauder Hunter station. "Briefing begins in one minute, twenty-four seconds."

She ignored the secretary and rushed to the locker room, pulled off her torn coat, and shoved it into a locker.

It was warm inside, and a faint smell of leather hung in the air of the Hunter's department. The office always smelled of leather. Every law enforcement agency wore specially crafted leather boots, but it was the embroidered teal coats that separated the GMH from the rest. That coat was missing from Orinthia's locker.

From the corner of her eye, she could see someone leaning against the wall. Orinthia did not bother to look as she said, "I hate when you watch me like that."

"And we hate when you're late," Adoracion said. She stood up straight and walked closer. Her brown hair was pulled into a tight ballerina bun, but even at full height, the bun barely reached Orinthia's chin. "If you were anyone else, we'd have tossed you out long ago."

"Technically, I was inside the department on time." Orinthia unbuttoned her shirt and donned a fresh one from inside her locker. "I was visiting mom."

"You were last to arrive. Everyone else had the ability to show up in uniform at the appropriate time. Mom will always be there. She isn't going anywhere. We have a job to do *here*." The tip of Adora's slender nose pulled down when she spoke. "Where is your uniform?"

"I haven't picked it up from the tailor's yet. Do you realize how much detail goes into those things?"

Her sister rolled her eyes and walked out of the room.

Orinthia childishly stuck her tongue out before checking herself in the mirror. Her long, wavy hair cascaded down the sides of her body, stopping at the bend in her arms. The silver strands stood out against the navy-colored shirt she wore. She adjusted the bell sleeves and high collar of her blouse, then patted the dust off her black slacks. Satisfied with her appearance, she left the room.

The voices of the other officers reached her before she entered the briefing room. Once inside, she could see four dozen of her fellow officers in their agency-issued, grey-and-teal uniforms. Most ate breakfast and talked amongst themselves. A few looked over notes and documents on their Port-Tabs. No one looked back at her or made any sign they noticed she had walked in.

Orinthia strode over to the far side of the hall where a service bot hovered around a table, tidying up the meal spread. She picked up a tray and added bits of whatever was left.

"Let's get everyone settled," Arsenio shouted from the podium at the front. His overly gelled, slicked black hair stayed firm as he eyed the room. He stood half a foot taller than his twin sister beside him.

The chatter died down and only the subtle sound of chewing and the rubbing of fabric could be heard. Orinthia found a seat near the exit and ate her meal.

"Welcome back, crew," Adoracion said as she waved her hand over the screen behind her. Two unfocused images of a ship scrolled across. Orinthia squinted and tried to make out what she was looking at. It was a dark, curved shape which, to her, resembled a blurry stingray with no tail.

"These were sent to us last night," Adora continued, "along with a few other reports claiming the *Fera* was spotted near the Moon."

Whispers spread through the room.

The crew of the *Fera* were some of the original marauders. Like most marauders, they were veterans who banded together after the war. These began making a name for themselves by attacking Earth Confederate ships over the course of five years. But unlike most other marauders, they only went after the government's ships.

They should be the military's problem, Orinthia thought.

Adora cleared her throat, calling the room back to attention. "These may only be rumors, but just in case, Arsenio and I will take a small crew to check it out later today."

"That means the rest of you are on call, so be prepared to cancel any plans you have," Arsenio added. He lacked the attractive features his family had inherited from their mother. He did not share the same nose as his twin or Orinthia, but rather their father's bulbous one sat planted in the center of his face. His eyes were also half an inch too far apart and his lips stretched across his face. "If the rumors are true, we'll follow the lead as far as it goes."

"It would take at least an hour for the rest of us to get to you if you get caught in a fight," Orinthia said with a bite of pastry in the side of her mouth. "The *Mathias* is too slow to catch up to a ship like the *Fera* if they try to outrun you. Taking a sloop along would be better."

"That's actually a great idea." Arsenio nodded.

Orinthia choked.

"Captain Kian, pull together your best officers. You'll follow behind in MHS *Daring*." He pointed to a Goloric in a captain's black and teal uniform. Kian's bright purple skin shifted to blue, indicating his excitement.

OUTRAGED, Orinthia stood up, her chair scraping against the tile, and stormed out of the room. *It was my idea*, she thought. *I should've been given a crew.*

She sat on a bench in the locker room. The sound of her weapon charging and winding down as she flicked the safety off and on masked the steps of her sister rushing in.

"I can't believe you did that," Adora shouted.

A low hum sounded inside Orinthia's head. "You know that isn't true."

"Fine, I *can* believe you did that. It's just like you to cause a scene in the middle of a briefing. Always needing the attention for yourself."

"I wanted that job," Orinthia said, not looking up as she continued to fiddle with the gun. "It should have been mine. There are two dozen more arrests to my name than Kian has."

"But *he* is dependable, Orinthia. His prisoners are still behind bars. He doesn't overstep his boundaries, and he is a captain. We want to give you the position. Do you know how embarrassing it is that you're still an officer and not a captain? Do you know the grief we get for letting you slide with things because you are family?"

Orinthia looked up to see Adora holding her hand out.

"Give me your gun and identification," Adora said. "I'm not dealing with insubordination anymore. You're fired."

The gun hung loosely at Orinthia's side as she jumped up. Her eyebrows crushed together. "I am your sister. You can't fire me."

"I can and I am. You have been nothing but problems since you were a child. If it wasn't for Father, we never would have hired you. But I'm done. Get your life together, grow up, and stop being so self-centered."

"You've never made an effort to like me." Orinthia shoved the gun into Adoracion's open hand. "Father gave you gifts but cursed me."

Adora said nothing for a minute. When she did, she spoke in a normal, almost sympathetic tone. "None of us asked to be reimagined the way we were. We just play the hand we are dealt and get on with life."

3

*E*ven in a loud bar full of arguments and laughter, Adora's words echoed through Orinthia's head. "None of us asked to be reimagined..." She grumbled and tossed the contents of her cup down her throat. The pale orange liquid burned its way down and hit her stomach. *What does she know? They were given...*

A fight broke out behind her, interrupting her thoughts. Someone stumbled into her, pinning her to the bar. She struggled to breathe and pushed her arms against the counter. With shaking arms, Orin heaved away from it, letting the body of whoever was on top of her tumble onto the seat she previously occupied. Orinthia rubbed her chest and looked around.

Men were shouting. Somewhere to her left, a table splintered, pieces of wood and metal scattered around the room. A large Vulcronian woman with a golden arm and two thick curved horns, lifted a chair above her head and tossed it across the room. Orinthia watched it fly and hit a hulking creature on the side. Though the impact made the chair break in two, the alien did not drop the steel tankard in its crystal hand and took another sip as if nothing happened.

Orinthia turned her attention back to the fight. It became obvious the stone man was not the woman's target because she lifted another stool and struck a different man in the chest. The force sent him backward into a group of onlookers behind him. They hollered and pushed him away.

Orinthia was about to turn and ignore the scene, but the man reached for his hip and light reflected off the weapon he drew. Instinctively, she raised an arm to her chest, swung it back out, and her forearm transformed into a silver blade. Within four steps, she cleared the distance between them. The man barely had time to lift his gun before she placed the tip of the blade under his chin.

"Drop it," she ordered.

A hush fell over the room. Every conversation stopped and all eyes were on her. The man released the blaster and it crashed to the floor near her feet. She stepped on it and dragged it away from him. With her sword still on his throat, she leaned down, retrieved the gun, and tucked it into her coat.

"That's mine now." She nodded toward the stowed gun. "I suggest you find somewhere else to drink, too."

The man glanced down at steel touching his skin, then back to Orinthia. He glared at her and growled, "She started it."

A low hum sounded inside her skull, like bees trapped in a jar. "Do I look like your mother?" Orin twitched her arm, making an indent in his skin. "I don't care who started it. You made this my problem, so I'm talking to you."

"What're you, a cop?" He curled his lip in disgust.

"You wish I was. They have rules to follow. I don't."

Not that she would not have done the same thing when she was one. But she was already out of a job, her credits were overdraft, and rent was past due for two months. There was not much left to lose.

Orinthia pulled away from him and lowered her arm. In a reverse motion, the blade retracted and she took a step back.

The man bellowed and lunged at her.

Her arms flew up and caught him behind the neck. With her own throaty yell, she yanked down and thrust her knee into his abdomen.

He yelped and doubled over onto the floor as she let go.

She stepped over him and walked to the exit. No one said anything or made a move to stop her, only parted out of her way when she got close.

"I'll be back when it's quieter in here," she said to the bartender on her way out.

The difference in light stunned her eyes. She assumed the sun had already set, but there it was, dipping behind the skyscrapers, casting a golden glow over the city.

Her city. District One of The New Cruces Republic, the city she lived in her whole life.

There was no attachment, though. No pride in living here. To her, it was the same as any other metropolis in the galaxy. Too loud and too crowded. Every spare surface had ads for one product or another. Traffic blocked the skies, and people rushed from one place to the next. It was a fine enough place to live, but she wanted more.

The door to the bar opened behind her. She turned around with arms crossed at her chest, thinking the man was coming back for a second round. To her surprise, it was the stone and crystal creature from that morning.

They stood on the pavement, staring at each other.

Orinthia waited for him to say something, anything, but he kept looking at her, as if studying her. Irritated, she moved to walk away.

"I paid your tab," he said.

"Excuse me?"

"You left without paying for your drinks, so I covered it." He shrugged.

"Were you watching me?" The gun was heavy in her pocket and she wondered if it would be of any use against him.

"I think everyone was watching you."

"I can pay for my own drinks," she said.

"But you didn't, did you? Don't think I didn't notice you took the perfect opportunity to walk out. Everyone was distracted and in shock. Why wouldn't you? It was a pretty slick move."

"Do you feel like I owe you now?" She tried to turn her words to venom, but they came out curvy instead. "First this morning and now this?"

"No," he said flatly.

"I'm not saying 'thank you,' if that's what you're looking for. You needn't take care of me. My bills are my own business and I didn't ask for help."

"Of course you didn't." He shook his head. "It wasn't out of pity or a favor. Merely a gesture of good will."

"Good will for what?" She squinted her eyes at him. The sun was almost all the way behind the buildings and the light teetered between night and day.

"I think we've shadowed this doorway for far too long." The man nudged his head behind him. "There is a restaurant a few streets away. You can eat or not, I don't care. But it's quiet and I'd like to talk to you."

She stood with her arms still crossed, weighing her options. Would he continue to follow her if she refused? "Fine."

4

*T*he pair walked through the city, pushing by the impossible number of people walking past them. Orinthia felt like a fish going upstream, and everyone else fought against her. A group of teenagers huddled in the middle of the path, looking at their PortTabs and giggling to each other. She crammed into the middle of them. One yelled at her for making their PortTab fall.

Orinthia and her leader exited the most congested part of town, away from the newer steel and glass sections. Eventually, they reached a brick building. A blinking neon sign shone brightly in the dim street, shadowed by the skyscrapers. It was surprising to see something like this still existed.

"How retro," Orinthia said out loud.

"Best food around, I swear." The stone man pulled the door open. Smells of spices and meat drifted out.

Some Hunters who did deep space tours came back with stories of wormholes that sucked in ships and spit them out somewhere else in time. She suddenly felt like one of those wormholes opened in front of her as they stepped through.

Retro was not the right word. Even her grandparents' generation had more modern establishments than the one before her.

A curvy android with mismatched parts stood behind the counter at the back of the restaurant. Her seams were rusted, which blended in with the burnt orange paint job. Bits of wire stuck out of her head, making her look like a woman with frazzled hair.

"Hey, honey", the bot said. Glad to see you back. Help yourselves to some seats." Her voice was robotic and tinged with a seductive tone.

Orinthia followed the giant man to a booth in the far back corner. She sat on the bench and scanned her surroundings. It was darker than most places she was used to, and antique bulbs illuminated the room with a yellow glow. She had only ever seen them in her textbooks in school and had imagined no one still used them, let alone knew where to buy one.

Whoever had repaired the android must have chosen the decor. The walls were lined with photos and paintings that matched no general theme. No one even took still pictures anymore. It was almost astonishing how old everything was.

"Eclectic, isn't it?" the alien asked.

She turned her attention back to him. "Who are you?"

"Thrutt."

"What do you want?" Orinthia folded her arms and leaned against the back of the seat.

"Well, food to start. I haven't eaten since this morning."

She opened her mouth to demand an actual answer but was interrupted.

"What will it be, dolls?" the android asked.

Orinthia gave the waitress a once over and noticed she had wheels for feet. They looked to be the newest part of her makeup and were in near pristine condition.

"Like what you see, honey?" The android cocked her hip and ran a metal hand down her side.

Orinthia crunched her face into a fake smile. "Not my cup of tea."

"I'll take an Andromeda special, please," Thrutt said, swinging his massive arm on the backrest. Anyone walking by would assume he owned the place by the way he commanded the room.

"I'm not staying long," Orinthia told the wait-droid, who shrugged and rolled away to deliver the order to the cook.

"Where did you learn to fight like that?" Thrutt asked when they were alone again.

"I'm an Earth Confederate spy," she lied.

"Well, as a *spy*, I assume you've been to space. And not on holiday to the Moon colonies. Real space. Away from your solar system."

"A few times." Orinthia tilted her head back and studied the man.

"Got any other tech beside the blades?"

She squinted at Thrutt. "Where are you going with this?"

"My employer is looking for recruits," he explained. "Those with special talents they'd like to use for profit."

"What kind of profit?"

He moved his arm from behind him, leaned forward, and put his elbows on the table. "The kind you only get in deep space. Specifically, by looting ships that don't belong to you."

"Marauders." The words made her dizzy. It was no longer her job to care if he was one or not. But did he know she had been a Hunter?

He dipped his head. "I hail from the *Fera*."

Her skin tingled and her mouth went dry. If he had followed her after their morning encounter, it could have been a trap. There was only one way to know for sure.

"Do you know who I am?" she asked, frozen until he answered.

"What kind of question is that?" He scoffed. "Are you implying you're too good for marauding?"

"Answer me. Do you know who I am?"

"No, I don't know who you are. Should I?"

"Have you seen me anywhere else besides this morning and now?" she demanded.

"Are you famous or something? No, I haven't." Thrutt huffed. "Look, I was trying to offer you a job. If you don't want it, fine. Don't make it weird."

Orinthia let out a sigh. Her head was silent. Though she regarded it as a curse, being a human lie detector helped her out of tight spots now and then.

"I've never met a marauder before." She shrugged. "You startled me, is all. Don't you usually kidnap and force others to join your crew?"

"Not if we don't have to. During a battle, maybe. But on land, we tend to scout out the potential."

"What makes you think your 'employer' would want me?"

"Our crew is made up of mostly former military personnel," Thrutt began. "And since weapon mods are outlawed for private citizens, there are only a few ways to get them if you're not a soldier. Seeing as you were tossing 'em back in the middle of a weekday, I assume you're either broke or a thief. Either way, you'd fit in well."

The wait-droid reappeared with Thrutt's food. She set it in front of him on the table. Steam wafted from the circular bun. A grey disk and some vegetables were stuffed in between the two shiny tan pieces of bread.

"I love ancient Earth culture," Thrutt said, looking down at his food.

"For someone who claims to not know me, you assume an awful lot about my life." Orinthia could feel the drinks spinning her head. The smell of the food turned her stomach.

Grease dripped down his clear hands as he took a bite of the sandwich. "Most people glance over minor details about a person. I've learned to read people and I'm usually right. So, am I?"

Orinthia said nothing. She thought about her answer. "My modification is military, but I am not. They were a gift from my father. He was a weapons designer during the war."

"Was he?" Thrutt tilted his head and drew his mouth down. "My captain would be very interested in seeing him."

"That would make one of us." Orinthia wrapped her arms together and looked away. "He hasn't been around for a while, and I don't care to know where he is."

Thrutt finished the last few bites of his meal and said, "I'm sure you have a busy night of doing whatever it is you do, so I'll make my offer quick. Would you like to join our crew? It pays decently and the living arrangements aren't bad. I can't promise every day is going to be enjoyable. There will be hard work, and being an outlaw isn't for everyone. But you'll see places you never thought could exist and meet creatures who only live in dreams."

The options ran through her head. Sure, she was a bit of a rebel, but becoming a marauder the same day she was fired from hunting them? That was extreme, even for her.

"Sorry," she answered. "It's going to be a 'no' for me."

"Can't say I didn't try." Thrutt stretched his arms. His knuckles grazed the ceiling. "If you change your mind, I'll be at the docks until dawn. Find me there."

$\mathcal{N}$ ight in the city mirrored the daytime. Droves of people rushing here and there. Couples walked close together, whispering to each other and laughing. Families exited eateries, and children ran circles around their parents. Groups of teenagers and young adults gathered around club posters, looking for where to spend their night out. Delivery bots rolled their way through the narrow maze. It was what normal people did on a normal night.

Orinthia hated crowds. They made her head hum constantly, since her mod was activated by just the sound. It detected the inflection in a person's voice, the way they breathed when they spoke or emphasized the wrong syllables. Almost two decades of hearing people speak trained her modification to detect all dishonesty.

The trip home was unpleasant to say the least. She was tired, hungry, and too sober to ignore the pain in her skull. For once, the sight of her apartment building brought comfort. She tapped her watch against the door, stepped in, and slammed it shut behind her. Like a switch, the humming stopped. The lobby was empty, and she could take a moment to enjoy the peace. She rolled her shoulders and stretched her neck to ease the tension built up in her muscles.

Worried a fellow tenant would appear and wishing the sound in her head to cease for the night, she moved to the lift and once again tapped her watch to the scanner.

A male face emerged on the screen. "Welcome, Miss Anton. There is a message from Bliss McDougle. It is marked urgent."

"What does she want now? Just open it." Orinthia huffed.

"Yes." The man's face faded and a woman's took his place.

"Orinthia," the video recording of Bliss, her superintendent, said, "Look, I can't say you've been a good resident, but you aren't the worst. That being said, your rent is overdue again. If I didn't have so many people on the waiting list, we could work out a deal. I need to fill out apartments with people who will actually pay. Sorry, but you've got a week to get out. After that, I'm shutting off your access and whatever is left in the apartment will be forfeited over to us. It's not personal. Well, maybe a little 'cuz you called me a…"

"Audio restricted," the man's voice said.

"…last week, but mostly we need the credits. Anyway, hope you work things out, but you can't live here anymore." The recording of Bliss ended and the screen changed back to the digital blue of the building's virtual doorman.

"There is another message available from an unknown subject. Would you like to hear the rest of your messages?" he asked.

Even if she heard the machine, she could not have answered. Orinthia stood in the lobby. Her body shook like the room had suddenly frozen over. It was unlike her to not have words. She was usually ready with an answer for everything but at that moment, she felt alone. Not alone. Alone was preferable. Alone was familiar.

She was an outcast.

Sadness overcame her for a moment. Silent tears dripped from her eyes and broke away. As quickly as her grief arrived, it was chased away by anger and resoluteness.

If no one wants me, fine, she thought. *Maybe I will accept what I am. Who I was meant to be. It's time to embrace the darkness I've avoided and live like those I've hunted for so long.*

Orinthia pressed a sleeve to her cheeks, dried her face, and opened the lift doors.

THE WALLS of her apartment felt closer than usual, almost as if they were constricting her and ready to push her out into the world. Her fingers burned, and she flexed them open and closed, standing in the studio she had called home for three years. It was the only place she had ever lived outside of her father's house.

A tall bed was pushed up against the window in the center of the room. Her pillows teetered over the edge, supported by the mess of blankets on the floor. City lights shone in from below. They went on for miles until they fell into the sea of black. There was nothing beyond the city but the space port and open desert.

On top of the dresser at the foot of her bed was a mountain of dirty dishes, which could have easily been put in the kitchen sink three feet away. Two of the drawers were open. Clothes hung out like a fabric waterfall suspended in time.

Her shoes were scattered on either side of a pile of a week's worth of unwashed laundry.

The only other door besides the entrance led to the bathroom, which contained its own disaster. It would not be featured in any style articles on the social nets, but she was comfortable in the mess because it was her mess.

She sat on the edge of her bed and kicked off her boots. The knee-high leather was the only part of the GMH uniform she liked. Looking around the room, she felt a hint of sorrow at the thought of leaving. Though it certainly had its problems, like the faulty plumbing and outdated appliances, it served as her sanctuary.

The memory of the argument she and her father had the day before he went missing soured the joy she found in the place. Frustrated, she decided staring at the walls would not get her away any faster. Thrutt said he would be at the docks until morning, so she only had until then to pack what she needed.

6

*L*ighting the apartment on fire before she walked out crossed Orinthia's mind, but she decided to stick to only one felony for the day. With a backpack filled with the few possessions she cared to take, Orinthia opened the door and stepped out without a glance behind her. She did not bother to close the door. If someone wanted to steal what was left, they could have it. She had no intention of returning.

The sun had not yet risen when she stood outside of her building. Most people were tucked away in their homes, still sleeping or getting ready. This was Orinthia's favorite time of the day. Empty streets meant she did not have to put in the effort to avoid people. Of course, she rarely saw the early hours. In fact, the only occasions she experienced early mornings were when she arrived home after long missions. The irony was not lost on her.

At the risk of starting another battle with her nerves, one she had fought through the night while packing, she took a deep breath and forced herself to move.

There was one stop she had to make first.

The dew wet her knees as she knelt in the grass. "Hi,

mom," Orinthia said. "I know I was here yesterday, but I wanted to say goodbye. Things aren't working out here with the family, and it's time I left. They don't want me, and I don't belong. Hopefully, I will come back and see you someday."

She hiccuped as she choked back a sob. "Please forgive me. I-I don't know if you'd be proud of me, but maybe you could at least understand."

With shaking hands, Orinthia reached out and touched the sides of her mother's gravestone. She pinched her lips together and gave a quick nod before standing up. Her chest was tight, but she ignored it and puffed her lips out with a pop. As fast as she could, she put distance between her and the cemetery, not daring to stay a moment longer in fear she would change her mind.

There is nothing for me here, Orinthia determined in her head.

A ONCE GRAND and imposing sign hung over the entrance of the dock. "Home of the world's first commercial spaceport." People were no longer impressed by its history. Civilians took to the stars and stretched their arms out across the universe every day, as they had done for over 500 years.

The spaceport was not like its ocean counterpart. Barren land surrounded it. Long strips of pavement spanned the desert for miles. Rows of concrete and steel platforms jutted off the ground, all at varying heights. And though the city had grown out from the port, desert was still desert. Dry, hot, and untouched for centuries.

Orinthia stood near a service shed and watched ships

load, looking for her ride out of Dodge. Sloops and freighters landed and launched dozens at a time. Passenger cruises and hobby crafts weaved in and out of the way of the larger ships.

Thrutt stepped out of a ship ten platforms from where Orinthia stood. He and another man, a human-looking man, stood side-by-side speaking to each other.

This new man was tall, but not as tall as Thrutt. His black hair was pulled into a low ponytail tied at his neck. Orinthia moved closer, clutching her bag.

"I wasn't sure you'd come," Thrutt shouted as she approached. A large grin spread across his face.

"*I* wasn't sure I would come," she said. Though her heart raced, she kept her voice steady.

"Glad to see you either way!" He clapped his heavy hand on her shoulder and knocked her a step forward. "Now, before you can board our ship, you need to speak with the quartermaster. He's the keeper of the code."

The man beside Thrutt held his hand out. He had an intricate tattoo of a compass on his palm. "Kos Rogue, quartermaster on the *Fera*. The marauder's code is like a contract. They are our rules, and we live and die by them."

"I thought we were just going to pillage and loot?" Orinthia said, ignoring his hand. "Now marauders have rules?"

Orinthia had heard of them before. Every ship had their own brand of code. Seeing as she was supposed to never have met a marauder, she had to play the part.

"We have more honor than we're given credit for." Kos pulled his hand back and stood with his shoulders stiff. His voice deepened as he spoke. "My crew are not some low life criminals that don't judge the value of life. We take great pride in our conduct."

Thrutt put himself between the two, creating a barrier.

"I'm sure she didn't mean to offend, Rogue. We may be honorable, but there are those who aren't, and that's what people know."

Kos relaxed his posture and tilted his chin down. "Right." He took a tattered brown book from his coat and opened it.

"There is no drinking aboard the ship at any time. If you are found drunk more than once, you will be stripped of your privileges and dropped at the nearest inhabited planet. Drinking and the use of any mind-altering substances must be done on shore leave. If you return to the ship intoxicated, you will be confined to your cabin until the effects are worn off."

He continued. "Any disputes between crew members are settled off the ship. Your crew is your family and must be treated like such."

Orinthia choked on a laugh. *If he only knew how my family treated each other,* she thought.

"Something funny?" Kos looked up with only his eyes.

"Nothing, nothing. Go on."

He lowered his eyes and cleared his throat. "If you are found fighting on board, both parties will be stripped of privileges and dropped at the nearest inhabited planet. All romantic relationships are forbidden between crew members. If you are found involved, you will be…"

"…Stripped of your privileges and dropped at the nearest inhabited planet," Orinthia finished his sentence. "So pretty much anything fun will get you kicked off the ship?" And she thought she had it hard as a Hunter.

"Don't like the rules?" Kos closed the book on his finger. "You're welcome to walk away now."

She sighed. "I've got nothing left to lose, I suppose. Are there any more rules?"

Kos spoke without opening the book again. "All members are equal aboard the ship and have equal say. Only during battle does the captain have final authority. Every mate must vote when called upon to do so, and a majority vote from the crew may override punishments. Do you agree?"

Seconds crawled by as she thought about what he said. There was still time to turn back and pretend nothing happened. Maybe if she played her cards right, Adora would allow her to have her job back. But no. It would only continue the cycle she was in, suffocating beneath the shadow of their accomplishments.

"I agree," she said.

"Hold out your hand." Kos said, pulling a dagger from his belt with one hand and flipping the book open again with the other. "You are hereby sworn in by blood as a member of the *Fera*." The blade sliced into her finger, and three drops of blood landed on the pages of the book.

Before she could yell at Kos, Thrutt already had the vial of blue liquid and poured a drop onto her finger. "Welcome aboard," Thrutt said.

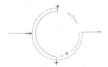

7

"*D*o either of you care that I have a name?" Orinthia looked at Thrutt who was replacing the container back into his coat. Not once in the time he spoke to her had he asked her name. He gave her his without hesitation the night before. Even Kos had an introduction. But not her.

"Most of us named ourselves," Thrutt said. "Marauders are generally running from something, usually a past they'd like to forget, or they have a family they'd like to protect. Either way, you're more than welcome to call yourself anything you'd like."

"We'll need to know what you choose eventually," Kos added. "But not until we get to the *Fera*. That will give you plenty of time to decide who you are. Get settled inside. We're taking off in five."

Orinthia watched him walk away. She hoped the *Fera* was big enough to avoid him.

"I'll show you around, come on." Thrutt ducked his head as he entered through the ship's bay doors. "This is one of two sloops we have. The *Fera* is too heavy to leave most atmospheres at any reasonable speed, so *Freya* does most of the back and forth."

"*Freya*?" Orinthia asked.

"She's the AI who runs the ship. I guess she *is* the ship. AI goes over my head."

"How does anything go over your head?"

"Tall jokes." Thrutt mocked offense. "So, original. Anyway, Rogue and she have been through everything together. She's about as reliable as he is."

Kos' voice came over the speakers. "Everyone better get strapped in. I will not be responsible for injuries this time."

Thrutt tossed his head for Orinthia to follow. They made their way through a narrow corridor to the seats. Five other marauders sat down before them.

The floor beneath her feet vibrated as the engines came on.

Orinthia settled into her seat next to a window and strapped the harness to herself.

Beside her, the seat creaked as Thrutt lowered himself in. "Don't look so nervous. Rogue is the best pilot in six galaxies."

"Is the *Fera* controlled by AI, too?" She scrunched her face. Artificial intelligence made her uncomfortable, especially when she was going to have to live inside something that could conceivably have its own thoughts.

Thrutt laughed. "No, Ahto controls her."

Ahto, the captain of the *Fera*. She had seen pictures and holograms of him, but only from his service days. "He's an Irelad, right? A sentient war machine?"

"Last one. But don't remind him of that. Most of us are trying to put those days behind us, but they are still very real for Ahto."

Orinthia preferred to drop it, anyway. Small talk was excruciating and left her drained.

The ship shook and the floor thumped as the landing gears disengaged. Faster and faster, the ship picked up speed and the passengers were pressed deeper into their seats. They swayed back and forth as *Freya* aligned herself on the right trajectory.

Gravity beat them into the seats. Orinthia's body felt heavy, like she doubled in weight every few minutes, until finally she could breathe without struggle. *Freya* won the battle against the laws of nature and they were in space.

Silver strands of Orinthia's hair lifted around her and floated up. Her harness was the only thing keeping her in one place.

"Auto grav initiated in 3… 2… 1…," Kos announced.

Before she could register what that meant, Orinthia felt her body again and fell gently into her place.

The Hunters kept the gravity turned on during launch. Their ships were larger and launched more like a balloon floating free than a slingshot. Most of the time, officers kept to their bunks during departure. Being weightless was a new sensation, and she could not say it was disappointing. Her heart pounded in her chest, and she wanted to feel it again.

Orinthia turned to face the window and watch Earth sink behind her. As she did, she wondered if she would ever return as she had promised.

"I thought you said you've been to space," Thrutt said. "You look like you've never seen your planet from up here."

She did not answer his question, only stared at the rock she had called home. The windows closed on their own and she could no longer see out. Orinthia pushed against the shutter, but it did not budge.

"They'll go back up when we come out of light speed,"

Thrutt said. "Too many sick accidents have happened from sailors looking out. *Freya* doesn't like the mess."

Another thought hit her, and though she wanted not to care, it made her sad. "No one knows I left," Orinthia said. What would Uri think when he came home and she was not there? Would he search for her? Would he worry? She left no note or message for him, only packed her things and disappeared into the cool morning.

"Well, you're not a prisoner," Thrutt said. "Next time we are in a port, you can send a message to tell them."

Orinthia chuckled at the idea of telling Uri she had run away to become a marauder. He would tell the twins and Adoracion would be livid. The red scar under her eye would burn as she yelled profanities into the air, angry Orinthia once again put a stain on the family's reputation.

THE TRIP LASTED AN HOUR. *Freya* slowed to a cruising speed, and Kos came over the loudspeaker again. "Approaching the *Fera* in two minutes."

Just as Thrutt had said, the ship's windows opened once again. Orinthia could not see where they were heading.

"You won't be able to make her out until we're closer," Thrutt told her. "She's the stealthiest ship ever made."

Orinthia recalled the photos from the day before, blurry and out of focus. "How?"

"That's more technical than I can explain, but the hull is made of metals extracted from asteroids. It helps her look like space junk on a radar and nearly invisible to the naked eye."

It made sense. The Hunters had multiple unclaimed bounties out for the capture of the *Fera*, but no one had been able to lay hands on it.

"There she is." Thrutt leaned over and pointed out the window.

Orinthia struggled to see anything but the void of space. She strained her eyes until a massive grey ship shifted into focus in front of her. Once she saw it, she wondered how she could have missed it in the first place.

Freya went around to the bow where the *Fera*'s bay doors opened like a mouth. Slowly, the sloop glided forward. The landing gears engaged and the floor beneath Orinthia shuddered as the weight of the ship settled.

"Home sweet home," Thrutt said.

8

*B*lack and yellow robots, no bigger than toddlers, rolled around the *Fera's* hold. They moved crates off *Freya* and placed them along the walls. The rest of the crew walked around them as if they were not there.

"Have you eaten yet?" Thrutt asked, breaking Orinthia's attention from the repetition of the bots.

Her stomach ached at the mention of food. She could not remember when she had eaten last. "No."

"I'll show you to the mess deck, then Kos'll get you situated with a cabin to set your things down." Thrutt led her away from the hold into the main body of the ship. She had to take two steps to his one just to keep up.

They walked by some of the crew on their way. A few of them glanced at Orinthia, but none stopped to say anything except for one dark grey creature.

"Glad you're back," it said to Thrutt. "You missed a good game."

Orinthia took a step to the side and tried to stay unnoticed. The universe had grown so much since Earth's first invasion, but old prejudices died hard. Chinda still made humans uncomfortable.

"I'm sure I did," Thrutt answered back. "I wasn't there to call you on your cheating."

They laughed for a second then continued on their way.

"He's harmless." Thrutt looked over his shoulder to Orinthia. "The fight was between your ancestors, not the two of you."

She scrunched her nose but did not say anything.

"Here we are," Thrutt said as he led the way through open doors. "Fresh meals are served two times a day, but self-service is always available."

Orinthia kept her head down while trying to watch the room for anyone who may have recognized her from her former life.

"You're welcome to try anything, but if you're not feeling adventurous, the Earth food is on the far right." Thrutt pointed to the end of the counter. "Cook likes to keep it separate from the rest of the food since humans have weaker systems than most of us."

That caught her attention. She sniffed and raised an eyebrow. "I'll take you up on that." Orinthia walked over to the spread and looked over her options. Other than water spheres and the so-called human food, she could not make out what was before her. Some of the meat was a color that turned her stomach. Others were cake-looking treats with fungus growing out the sides.

She grabbed a water sphere, a fungus cake, and some purple-colored fruit that jiggled when touched.

"You sure about those?" Thrutt asked. "Have you have ever had non-Earth food?"

Orinthia shrugged. "Can't be any worse than what my sister used to cook."

Thrutt chuckled and grabbed a tray with a few bits of his own. He nodded his head for her to follow, and they sat down at a table with a few other crew mates.

Orinthia placed her tray down and assessed what she took. From the side of her eye, she could see an orange creature with four arms staring at her. She lifted her head to meet its gaze. She would not be intimidated or show any weakness on her first day. If she were going to survive in this new world, she would have to prove she belonged. "What are you looking at?" she asked the creature.

Thrutt leaned in beside her. "Don't mind him. His translator chip got damaged a few days ago. He needs to get it fixed, but he's wanted on several planets in this region, so it's going to be awhile."

Orinthia gave a quick nod. "Happened to me once. Got kicked in the side of the head when I was trying to apprehend a-…" she stopped herself from saying 'fugitive.' "Anyway, my ear didn't stop ringing for a week." She thought of that week fondly. The twins made her stay home alone in her quiet apartment until she could get the chip replaced. It was better than any vacation she ever took with her family.

"You really gonna eat that?" a female Arachnillo asked. Her pedipalp rubbed together as she examined the newcomer. She folded four of her arms in front of her on the table.

Orinthia looked down at her food and wondered the same thing. Maybe eating random food was not the best way to test the waters, but she was already committed and had to see it through. She did not answer, only picked up the cake and took a bite. It squirted inside her mouth and bile raced up her throat. She fought through the urge to spit it out and continued to eat the squishy bits in her mouth. Her tongue felt fat and she was not sure if she was having an allergic reaction or her body was fighting to keep her from swallowing. After much chewing, she forced it down but could not fight the shiver as it landed in her nearly empty stomach.

A burp slipped from her mouth. "Well, that was unpleasant."

"This one is humpage." The Arachnillo used one of her pointed hands to point at the jiggling meat. "It's a sweet fruit from my planet."

Orinthia lifted it and watched it dance in her hands. It did not resemble any fruit she had ever seen, but then again, the twins never let her leave the ship when they made port. There was an entire universe she had never experienced, and eating weird food was part of that. She took a bite. Her eyes widened and jaw tingled. A sour juice spilled down the sides of her chin. It did not taste like anything she could describe, but she wanted more. Each bite sent her jaw tight, but the flavor was overwhelming.

"Good, yes?" The Arachnillo smiled, revealing her fangs.

Orinthia wiped her face on the back of her sleeve. "I wouldn't call it sweet, but I also wouldn't refuse more of them."

"Xyla, Gunner first class," the Arachnillo introduced herself.

Orinthia responded with a smile. She had yet to decide on a name that suited her. Assuming she had more time to come up with one, she leaned back in her seat and sipped her water sphere.

9

"*C*aptain on deck," Kos announced.

Orinthia had registered heavy footsteps followed by quick lighter ones. She glanced back to see two men walk in. Kos Rogue followed a pace behind a tall, pale man. The other man walked with his back straight and his arms behind his back. His navy-blue coat was buttoned and straight, resembling that of an Earth Confederate officer. It was unmistakable who he was.

Thrutt gave her a nudge and she realized she was the only one still sitting. *I thought I left all the protocols and rigidness on Earth.*

"At ease, please." Ahto spoke so his voice traveled through the room. It was clear and commanding and set a stiffness in Orinthia's chest. "Rogue, do stop announcing my entry into every room. We are no longer chained to old authorities."

Kos shrunk back a hair and lowered his chin. "Aye, sir."

Ahto sighed. He and Kos stopped in front of Orinthia. "You must be the new recruit. What a pleasure. I am Captain Ahto."

Orinthia gave her hand and he clasped his firmly around it. "Thia," she said impulsively. It was the name her brother Uri used for her, and it felt safe and familiar in her ears as she said it out loud. "It is an honor to meet you, sir."

Ahto grinned. His teeth were unnaturally smooth, like whoever designed him had not intended him to smile often. "Most people are either unaware of who I am or completely terrified. How is it you are neither?"

"I've followed your career for a while. There're a few people back on Earth who will be upset I'm standing here with you," Orinthia said. She took pleasure in knowing exactly what she said was the truth, just not in the way he would understand it. "I feel like I know you already."

Captain Ahto returned his hands to his back. "Let's hope there are still a few of my secrets left hidden. No matter. It's my pleasure to welcome you aboard the *Fera*." He lifted his head to acknowledge Thrutt. "Remember, you are responsible for her. Her failures are your failures, so push her to perfection."

Thrutt nodded. "Yes, Captain."

"Quartermaster Rogue will show you to your cabin," Ahto spoke to Orinthia again. Her attention jarred by the swiftness of the conversation. "Anything you need will be funneled through Thrutt. Oh, and do find yourself a new wardrobe. No need to dress like a common fool. You're a marauder now, might as well look the part."

Ahto turned on his heels without another word and marched out of the hall.

"When you're ready," Kos said, stepping to the side and holding a hand out toward the exit.

Orinthia almost forgot he was there. He was slender and tall but blended into the background with ease.

There was no use in waiting around. She picked up her pack and followed Kos.

THE CREW QUARTERS were two levels down from the main deck. Their footsteps were more muffled than they had been on the upper decks. Was it because there was more mass around them to absorb the sound, or was it planned that way for comfort of the residents behind the doors? Orinthia was not sure, but did not mind a quiet space to live in.

"This will be your cabin," Kos said after they walked half the length of the corridor. "I've already added your profile to the system, so you'll be able to move freely about the ship. If a door doesn't open, you weren't meant to be there."

Orinthia felt exposed. Her heart rate sped up and she rubbed her finger with her thumb where the blade had cut. "Did you use my blood from the ledger?" she snapped her words at him.

Kos pulled his head back, as if he could not see why it was even a question. "Yes. That's part of why I take it."

"Don't do that again," she blurted. "At least have the decency to let me know beforehand."

He held his hands up. His eyebrows tightened. "Alright."

Thrutt cut through the tension, like a parent trying to stop a fight before it happened. "You just have to walk up to the doors and they'll open. Try it."

Orinthia gave Kos a glare from the side of her eye as she turned and faced the door. She took a step forward and it slid open on its own. The inside was bare other than a cot with folded sheets and a table beside it. Across from the bed, though, left her speechless.

A window spanned a quarter of the space and reached from the floor to the ceiling, exposing the whole of the galaxy. Stars as far as she could see. No matter how many times she had seen space, it still blew her away.

"You'll have to see the observation deck," Thrutt said, standing beside her. "After you get settled in, I'll show you around. We'll get you changed first."

She looked up at him. The fire in her chest a moment ago fizzled away. "I think what I brought falls under the 'common fool' category."

"Not a problem," Thrutt said. "A benefit of living as a marauder, you take the spoils of battle. Including tech. A year after we began marauding, but before the *Fera* was built, we ran across an EC ship. After an hour-long battle, their captain surrendered to save his crew. As part of negotiations, they were shuttled off in an escape cruiser and left the ship for us."

He moved to the wall on their left and waved his hand. The panel opened and clothes sprung up out of the floor before him.

"Luckily for us, their captain was vain and had fitted a system that would allow him to call any piece of clothing he wanted. Our engineer stripped it, and when the *Fera* was complete, we integrated it into her mechanics. You use it the same way as the doors. Step close, and it will send up clothes based on your species."

Orinthia did not like the ship having so much information on her but found the idea interesting. Thrutt moved out of the way to allow her a try.

"I think I can manage from here," she said. "You two don't…"

It was only Thrutt standing in the room with her.

"Where did he go?" she asked.

"Rogue doesn't stay in one place too long," Thrutt

answered, not turning to see who she was talking about. "He's there one minute and gone the next."

"Well, you don't have to wait around while I change."

"Can't do. I have to make sure you're not hiding anything," he said with a straight face.

Her mod told her he was lying. She glared at him.

"I'm only kidding." Thrutt let out a booming laugh. "You should see the look on your face." He made for the door and waved a hand behind him. "I'll be back later to give you the rundown of the ship."

10

*O*rinthia stood in her sparsely furnished room, with her pack clutched tightly in her hands. It was silent. Not even the ship's engines could be heard. The lack of sound was heavy on her ears, but like a thick blanket on a chilly night. Comforting. If she had to imagine heaven, it would be this. Though the space needed work, she was content.

Her arms ached from holding the satchel. Finally alone, she set it on the bed, opened it, and laid out its contents.

Clothes that were no longer necessary, the blaster she took from the drunk at the bar, a bottle of scented liquid, and at the bottom of the bag, a framed photo. She held it in her hands for a minute, looking over the details she had memorized every night for twenty years.

It was the only photo she had of her and her mother alone. Orinthia found it while hiding from Adora, who had been furious at Orinthia for telling their father she lied about sneaking out through the observatory window. The memory threatened to flood her, but she shoved it away, focusing on the image in her hand.

Jean and Orinthia sat smiling. Both had the same auburn

hair and dimple on their left cheeks. Orinthia's hair would not change for a few years, a side effect of the modification her father implanted. A visual reminder of her curse.

She set the frame on the desk and pressed the screen. The photo came to life. "Look at the camera, sweetie," her mother's voice said. "Say 'Hi, daddy.' We love you, sweetheart. I hope you enjoy getting messages from each of the children this year. Happy birthday."

The image went still again. Jean and baby Orinthia sat frozen in time. She always imagined her mother was speaking to her, and not her father.

Orinthia took shallow breaths and pushed the ache down, opened the drawer, and put the photo facedown inside.

She blinked hard and looked at the closet, still full of the clothes it had summoned for her. From where she sat, everything looked dark and brooding. *Just because I'm depressed doesn't mean I have to dress like it,* Orinthia thought.

With a sigh of defeat, she stood and rummaged through the coats. When she pushed the last one aside, they retreated into the floor, and several more took their place.

"Now this is more like it," she said, picking up a pastel pink waistcoat. She pressed it against her body and looked down to examine how it looked. "Perfect. Now, I need pants."

As if the machine heard her, which she thought it probably had, the shirts and coats dropped and were replaced by a variety of bottoms. Long skirts, short skirts, britches, tights she could not imagine anyone squeezing into, and lastly, a pair of blindingly white officer pants.

"That's the one." Orinthia took the white pants from the rack and draped it over her arm along with a high collared white blouse and the coat. With her outfit complete, she stepped away from the closet and the paneling closed, drawing the leftovers down as it did.

Orinthia opted to keep her knee-high Hunter boots. They were specially made for her feet, and she doubted she would find anything more comfortable. "I'm sure no one will notice."

As she dressed, Orinthia tossed her old clothes on a pile near the door. When she was finished, she moved back and faced the window again. This time using it as a mirror, focusing on her own reflection, and turning from side to side. Satisfied with what she could see, she made for the door and walked out.

Thrutt said he would come back for her but having him hover over her another minute longer was not how she wanted to spend her first day as a marauder. Her feet bounced as she stepped into the lift. A new life waited for her and she was ready to dive in.

When the lift opened at the main deck, Orinthia poked her head out and looked to see if anyone was around. A group of marauders stood talking to her left. This prompted her to go right instead. She moved through the ship, noting the rooms that opened to her as she passed. Each time she came to a split in the corridor, she again gauged which way would be less occupied and went that way.

This method served her well until the corridors seemed to multiply. Some narrowed and she pressed herself against the wall to move through. Others were wide enough for four Thrutts to walk side by side. She could not understand where any of them led, and she felt lost.

How is it possible to have so many directions on such a small ship? she wondered. Even the twins' mile long flagship, the MHS Mathias, was easier to walk across.

After going for what she thought was hours, she found herself stepping into a massive open space. The room was dark at first, and she assumed she had walked into another wide hall. Then the ceiling opened above her.

She drew in a gasp of hair and held her breath, throwing herself back the way she came, fearing she would be sucked out the opening and float away. When that did not happen, she exhaled and ventured inside, stepping lightly.

This must be the observation deck Thrutt mentioned, she thought. Though the view from her room was breathtaking, this was awe-inspiring.

A set of stairs led up to a second, balcony-like level. Orinthia climbed the steps, not once looking away from the ceiling. She gently glided across the landing and stared. Her mouth fell open. Feet above her was the whole of the universe. Galaxies and stars spiraled and twinkled through the crystal-clear glass.

The sight mesmerized her, and she longed to reach out and grab hold. Her back bumped the railing.

If only I could get closer, Orinthia thought. Putting a foot on the edge of the banister, she lifted herself up and stood on top. Her toes bore the weight of her body as she stretched as far as she could. The dome was cool against her fingers as they grazed the glass. She let her head fall back and take it all in, refusing to blink in fear of missing a moment.

The *Fera* sailed along the edges of a tadpole galaxy. Two galaxies collided together. The tail end of the smaller one swung around the larger as it was ingested, leaving a trail of stars and space dust in its wake.

Someone walked into the room. Their footsteps startled her. Orinthia lost her balance and, as if she were floating, hung in the air for a moment before falling back. The view widened as she dropped away from the glass onto the level below her.

11

"**W**hat the…"

Orinthia crashed to the deck and huffed as the air left her lungs.

Kos rushed to her and looked over her, his mouth open and hands out. Confusion and panic crossed his face. "What just happened? Are you okay?"

She coughed and wiggled her toes inside her boots.

He brushed the hair off the side of his face and revealed a tattoo on his temple. Kos pressed two fingers against it. A translucent shield appeared, covering his eyes. He looked her up and down. "Nothing looks broken." He tapped the tattoo again, retracting the glass. "What were you doing up there?"

Orinthia rolled to her knees and stood up. She glanced back to where she was a moment before. The tadpole galaxy had passed and there was nothing but flecks of light against the black canvas.

"I was giving myself the grand tour," she answered, looking at Kos. "But I got lost."

"Why didn't you call a service bot?" he questioned.

"Right? I should have known that since I've been here for all of five minutes."

Kos fidgeted with his teeth against his bottom lip. "Oh, yeah. Well, the *Fera* was designed to misguide those who don't know her. Ahto planned it that way to keep us safe from Hunters and other enemies."

The mention of Hunters made Orinthia's heart seize. She changed the subject. "Why is Ahto *that* way?"

Kos creased his eyebrows.

"Irelad were built to take orders. I mean, I know they are AI, but weren't there safeguards put in place to keep them from going off the leash?"

He chewed the inside of his lip like he was conflicted about answering her question. "I've served with him a long time and fought beside him in war. I will not speak ill about my captain."

Orinthia smiled, knowing she pressed a button he did not like, but left it alone for the time being. "So, you were a soldier?"

Kos gave her a curt nod. "Navigator in the Earth Confederate Space Navy."

Orinthia noticed his hands tug at the sleeves of his coat. Her heart softened toward him. "How many mods do you have?"

He looked at the ceiling and murmured, "Five."

"How many of them did you ask for?" She was almost whispering.

"The only decision you make when joining the military is enlisting," he said, as if quoting someone from long ago. "You are property of the EC until discharged or killed in combat."

Orinthia scrunched her face and blew air out of her nose. Her heart rate picked up and it surprised her to feel anger toward those who mistreated someone who annoyed her so much. If asked, she would take pride in not knowing about the war. But she understood enough to know soldiers were property.

Kos looked at her like he was seeing her properly for the first time. His brown eyes were rimmed with green, and quickly moved back and forth over her face. "It's not all bad. At least they let me keep them. I'm sure they assumed we would re-up our contracts after the war ended."

"Why didn't you?"

His face turned dark, like he saw an old advisory walk in. "I should get a service bot to help you back to your room so you don't get lost again." He moved to the wall and waved his hand near a grey panel. A mono-wheeled yellow and black bot, like the ones she had seen in the loading bay, rolled out.

"Yes, Quartermaster Rogue?" A blue line jumped and moved as the machine spoke. "How may I assist you?"

"Escort Thia back to her cabin, please. She's had a fall, so take your time."

"Aye, aye, sir." The bot turned and faced Orinthia. "Follow me."

"Um, thanks," Orinthia said to Kos.

He gave her a half smile, but his eyes seemed to look somewhere far away.

The bot rolled away the way she came in.

Orinthia followed it, but the aching in her back slowed her down. "He said take your time, bot." She huffed.

"There is no concept of time in my data," the bot spoke, continuing at a brisk speed. "Robots are not living; therefore, time is irrelevant."

"Yeah, yeah," she said, trying to keep up with the miniature robot. "Then it shouldn't matter if you go fast or slow."

The bot halted. "Accurate. But my programming also dictates efficiency." It rolled away again, though a little slower than before.

The journey was quicker than when she did it on her own. They passed fewer corridors, moved through doors she had not seen before, and ended up at the lifts in no time at all.

Orinthia was glad to see the door open to her cabin when they finally stopped. The bot glided to an opening in the wall, rolled in, and was closed in behind the metal once again. She wondered where everything, like the crew's clothes and the bots, went when they slipped in like that. But she did not care for long. Her back was sore from the fall and made worse by the marathon she had run to get back to her room.

The cot gave a little as she laid down. She stayed still and let the pain release from her body. While she did, she thought about the day she had. It was hard to believe it all fit in the same day. Less than twenty-four hours before, she had disarmed a man in a bar, walked out on a tab, and been left wondering what she was going to do next.

Orinthia could not tell if it was the fall or the whiplash of events, but her head spun. Then she smiled. Not a full smile, like waking up to a hoverboard on the morning of her tenth birthday, but one of contentment. For the first time in twenty-one years, no one knew of her mod. No one could abuse or take advantage of it. And though she was not sure what time it was, or how long she had been away from Earth, she closed her eyes and let the peace of her new home come over her.

*a*larms blared and lights flashed. Orinthia gasped and sat up from her cot. The pain in her back had ebbed while she slept, but the quick movement made her stiffen. She pressed a hand to her side and stood up.

"All hands on deck," a voice shouted over a speaker she could not find. "Approaching EC cargo ship. Going half burn until target is within range."

The lights continued to flash as she focused on what was happening. Were they being attacked? She had not felt any cannon fire hit the ship. Orinthia looked to the side table, reached in the drawer for the blaster, and put it on her hip.

There was a knock on her door.

Taking her coat from off the foot of the bed, Orinthia moved to the doors. Thrutt stood on the other side, grinning.

"You ready?" he asked.

Orinthia looked down the hall. Marauders filed out of their cabins toward the lift. "I'm not sure what's happening," she answered.

"We've been cruising toward a lesser traveled EC

freighter route," he explained. "One's come close enough for us to ambush."

"I thought we were supposed to vote or something." Orinthia tried to recall what Kos had said through her haze.

Thrutt backed away from the door into the center of the hall, motioning for her to join him. "That happened a few days ago. There have been a few on our radar and we were waiting for the right moment."

Orinthia shrugged on her coat and fell in beside Thrutt. They loaded into the lift with four other crew members and rode it to the main deck.

"Stay with me," Thrutt said as they exited.

"I don't need a babysitter." She pressed her lips together into a thin line. This would be the first action she had, and she was eager to prove herself.

"Not for your safety. It's my duty as your sponsor to keep an eye on you and show you how this is going to go. We don't need you killing any one of us unwittingly."

Orinthia popped out her lips. "For marauders, you sure have a lot of rules."

"We aren't anarchists," Thrutt said. "Like I said, most of us served in the military at one point or another. Rules are comfortable and keep things going smoothly."

She did not understand, but let it drop. They caught up with the rest of the crew in the loading bay. Fifty marauders stood around, bouncing on the balls of their feet, stretching, and talking loudly to each other. Their voices echoed through the air.

Thrutt said something she could not make out. Her mod was humming in her head and it compounded the dizziness she had already felt from jumping out of bed.

I did not think this through, she told herself. *Of course marauders are a bunch of liars. What did I expect?* Orinthia wanted to cover her ears and scream for them to shut up.

"Then the doors will open and we'll board their ship." Thrutt's voice broke through the commotion.

Orinthia looked up at him, trying to recall anything he had said up until that point.

"Half a dozen or so will stay behind in case anyone tries to come on our side," Thrutt continued, unaware she had not heard the previous information. "If that happens, we'll get notified through the comms."

"What comms?" A wave of heat rushed through her, like she missed part of her uniform and was about to be scolded.

"You haven't been assigned one yet," Thrutt answered. "Logistics or something, I don't know. The techs don't like to give newcomers equipment in case they desert, get killed right away, or on the off chance they turn out to be a Hunter."

Orinthia let out an involuntary panicked laugh. "Has that happened before?"

"Only once. But Ahto weeded him out quickly and dealt with it." Thrutt shrugged as if it was not a big deal.

"What happened to him?" Her cheeks burned as if she had suddenly gotten too much attention. *You're not a Hunter*, she repeated in her head.

He opened his mouth but was unable to answer. From somewhere above them, the voice, which Orinthia recognized as Kos, shouted, "Master Gunner, ready the ion cannon. Gunners, prepare your boarding parties. We'll come along their port side in five minutes."

Thrutt leaned in. "That's us."

Xyla approached. She wore a high-collared grey vest that stood out against her shimmering blue exoskeleton. "Ready for some mayhem?" She addressed Orinthia. "Stay close to

Thrutt. If you get separated, find me. But don't wonder off on your own. We stick together, we stay alive."

She then faced Thrutt. "Our team is set to secure the cargo and get it ready for transport. When that's done, you two will return here and escort Gates and his team back to retrieve it."

Once again, Xyla looked at Orinthia and smiled. "See you when you get back. Have fun but stay alert." She gave Orinthia a pat on the shoulder and walked back, presumably to give the same instructions to the rest of her unit.

Orinthia rubbed her hands against her pant legs. Her head hummed and back ached. Bile built up in her throat. She felt unprepared and out of place. *This was a bad idea.*

Thrutt must have read her face. "Hey, this is going to be a textbook raid. We'll be in and out before you notice. Generally, they surrender and let us take what we came for without a fight because they know the shipment isn't worth their lives."

His words were soothing, and though he was made of stone, he had a delicateness to his voice.

The ship jolted, sending Orinthia off balance. She reached out and grabbed Thrutt's arm, who in turn steadied her.

"That was the ion cannon," he explained. "It packs a punch, but only to their defenses. We don't destroy ships unless we have to." Thrutt did not release her arm, though she pulled back.

When the second shock came, she understood why.

"That's them firing back."

The volley continued for several minutes until the ship stilled. She waited a few breaths and decided the EC ship must have been disabled. Her suspicions were confirmed when the bay doors opened.

13

*T*he air was alive with anticipation. Energy surged in waves off everybody in the crowd. Clothes rustled. Someone stomped and chanted. It was the breath before a leap.

Orinthia stood in the back, away from the doors. She watched as the mouth of the bay opened, exposing the blackness of space. Three looters dressed in full spacewalk gear hopped from the exit. Once free of the air seal, they lit their booster packs and made for the EC's damaged ship.

From where Orinthia stood with Thrutt, she could not see how far they went, or what they did when they got there. She lifted herself up with her toes and craned her neck, but it was no use.

"They're breaching the cargo hatch to create a connection with a gangplank between the ships," Thrutt explained. "That way we can go over without the need of our own spacewalk suits."

It made sense. Orinthia had given no thought as to how they all would get into the ship, which made her feel foolish. The feeling passed quickly when she heard a heavy explosion from outside the ship. Her mind's eye pictured the three marauders blown off the ship, sent to drift into the vacuum of space.

"Connection established," a voice called over Thrutt's comm. It was a universal announcement to the whole landing crew. "Extending air seal in 3… 2… 1…"

The air grew thin for a few breaths, then normalized again as the inhabitable bounds of the *Fera's* barrier reached out and attached to the ship across from them. Teams left the ship one shift at a time. In minutes, only two squads were left.

Orinthia followed Xyla's lead out onto the newly formed causeway. She looked around as they exited. The shield holding the oxygen in was as invisible as the air itself. Below her was a foot wide steel platform that unfolded out from the docking bay of the *Fera*. There was a chill over the walkway, but not unbearable. The closer they moved toward their objective, the bolder Orinthia grew. The nerves she had pent up back in the bay were loosening. She was ready to complete her first task as a marauder.

The area they entered was empty. Orinthia could hear shouting deeper inside the ship, but she could not tell what they were saying or whose side they were on. Her hand rested on the blaster at her hip, ready to draw if the moment came, though she was not looking forward to killing anyone. It was the one part she avoided thinking about.

In the years she served as a Hunter, she never took a life. Wounded? Sure. The adrenaline from a good fight was the only high she was allowed. But her prisoners had a jury to face and were no good to anyone dead.

"Where are you going?" Thrutt broke through her thoughts.

Orinthia snapped back to the present and realized she was

standing alone. He waved his clear hand at her and she hurried to join him.

"You going to be able do this?" he asked when she caught up.

"I'm fine. Just got distracted," she snapped.

Thrutt held up a hand to placate her. "I only wanted to make sure. You're favoring your left side when you move."

She did not think anyone would notice. "It's nothing. Let's get this done."

The two of them rejoined their team of six and closed the rear. They stopped outside a set of glass sliding doors.

"After you." Xyla gestured to Thrutt.

He stepped up and pressed his fingers against the panes, and turned like he was trying to twist unseen doorknobs. The glass screeched as he applied more and more pressure, continuing to rotate his hands in circles. With a final push, two round slabs fell out of the doors.

Thrutt stuck his arms into the opening and pulled back until they gave way and parted enough for the crew to enter. He stepped back and waited for the others to go through before he fell in line.

Seven EC sailors stood in the center of the hold with their fingers laced above their heads and blasters on the ground in front of them.

Xyla waved one of her hands and two of her team members rushed in and confiscated the weapons on the floor. Another two members drew out their blasters and held them facing the surrendering crew.

"The rest of you, start tagging the crates and ready them for transfer," Xyla ordered. "We have roughly ten minutes before their ship pings again and Command realizes they haven't moved."

Thrutt led Orinthia away and handed her flashing dots.

"Put these on anything that says 'ID 848'." It was the only instruction he gave her before moving on to start his own labeling.

Tagging crates was not the excitement she expected. The blaster weighed on Orinthia's belt. She had not had a chance to fire it since she disarmed its previous owner and was itching for an opportunity.

Orinthia used up all her tags within two minutes. She looked back at Thrutt and was made to go back for more. Something caught her eye before she completed a step. A silhouette of a human shadow darted across the wall. There were no humans on the landing team aside from her.

She unlatched her gun from its holster and moved quietly around a crate. Before she could raise her weapon, an over-looked sailor dove out from behind a box and slammed into her. They fell to the ground. The pain in Orinthia's back shot through her.

Her attacker was on top. He lifted his hand to swing at her face. With the movement of freeing her hand, she moved her blaster to his gut and pulled the trigger. His eyes widened, and he gasped in shock.

Nothing happened.

Again, she squeezed the trigger. Nothing.

The young sailor swung down and contacted her cheek.

Orinthia could taste the metallic sensation of blood as her teeth dug into the sides of her mouth. She lay dazed on the floor but managed to yell out.

Within seconds, Xyla rushed to her. Orinthia could see her paces away, her blaster drawn.

A flash followed by a crack ripped through the air. Xyla froze mid-stride and clutched her middle. Another flash and crack. The Arachnillo drew in a hollow breath and fell over.

Shouting echoed around the bay. Orinthia could not make

sense of who was saying what. All she could concentrate on was the black goo oozing from her Gunner.

Thrutt joined her and rushed the sailor before he could fire another shot. He clocked the sailor in the jaw. The young sailor went down without a fight.

Orinthia rolled onto her stomach, wincing at the ache in her back exacerbated by the fall she had, and pulled herself to her feet. She could not look away from Xyla, whose eyes were wide and mouth set as a permanent gasp.

"We have to go," Thrutt said, moving past her.

"What about her?" Orinthia's focus drifted up to Thrutt. "Wait, why are you carrying him?"

14

*O*rinthia stood with her arms tight around her chest and watched as they dragged Xyla's lifeless body back onto the *Fera*. No one looked at her or said a word. It was as if she were part of the wall, which was fine with her. She drew in deep breaths through her nose and only exhaled when her lungs shook.

"We only got half the crates," someone spoke over a comm. "There's no time to get the rest."

"Hurry and get back," another voice said. Orinthia could not tell who was speaking or whose comm it came from. "Command is contacting the ship. It won't be long before those sailors in the bay wake up and spill what happened."

"Copy." The comm went silent again.

Orinthia's head was spinning. She never experienced a casualty of a fellow Hunter while on duty. And it was the first time she watched the light drain from someone's eyes.

"Take him to the brig," Thrutt said.

Orinthia moved her eyes enough to see him pass the unconscious sailor who attacked her over to the Chinda she saw earlier. Thrutt then rubbed his face before facing her.

"Are you hurt?" he asked.

The ache in her back was constant, but she shook her head.

"Explain what happened."

Orinthia ran through the details, pausing when she reached the point where Xyla was laid out on the ground.

Thrutt pressed his fingers to his forehead. Even in her half aware state, Orinthia found it odd that he made such a human action.

"We need to get you cleaned up and ready," he said, putting his hands to his side.

"Ready for what?" Her voice was hushed and raspy.

He did not answer.

Orinthia followed him back to her cabin. She stepped in first and sat on her bed. Her hand moved to the drawer but stopped before opening it.

Thrutt leaned against the wall and stared out the window into space. The *Fera* had already left the EC ship by the time they reached her room.

The silence was thick, and for once, it made Orinthia uncomfortable. "Ready for what?" she repeated.

"We have a tradition. If someone dies coming to the aid of another, the surviving party must avenge the fallen." He spoke slowly and clearly.

"I have to…" Orinthia let the words fill her mouth, "…kill him?"

Thrutt nodded. "Fight him to the death, to be more specific."

All the air in her chest rushed out, and she struggled to regain control. Her mod made no sound. He *was* telling the truth.

Orinthia opened the drawer and drew out her mother's picture. She prayed the words Jean spoke would change and she would tell her what to do. Jean's voice filled the room. Orinthia had never let anyone see the photo let alone listen to its message. But she needed comfort, whether Thrutt was there or not.

"Who is that?" Thrutt asked in a hushed tone.

She stared at the woman on the screen. Her eyes unfocused and Orinthia's own reflection blinked back. "My mother and I."

"When did you lose her?" He did not move closer, but Orinthia could hear him change his stance.

"I was four." Orinthia's throat grew tight. "She and my oldest brother were walking home from the shops when a demolition was about to happen. They and thirty others stopped to watch. Someone mis-wired the explosives. When they blew, pieces of the building catapulted into the street. Half of the people were killed including my mother. She shielded my brother with her body."

"I'm sorry." Thrutt took soft steps toward Orinthia and touched her shoulder.

She did not pull away. "It shouldn't bother me as much as it does. I never knew her. But I also feel like part of me is missing because of it." Though her heart ached, she felt a weight lift off her chest. Most people did not like when she spoke about Jean, especially those within her family. The pain of death made the hearers uncomfortable, and she learned to keep her sorrow private.

"Long before your war began, another war happened on my planet. My division was on deployment. While I was off fighting, our home was left unprotected and our enemies invaded. They slaughtered millions of my people, along with my wife and three children. It's been a hundred years since I held them."

Orinthia looked up to face him. "One hundred? You're not that old."

Thrutt gave her a side smile. "I'm over two hundred years old."

The mod in her head stayed quiet while he spoke, and unless it received damage during either of her falls, she knew he was not lying. "How did you get over the hurt?"

"Didn't. I'm not sure those wounds heal. They just get easier to live with and hide. Time goes on and you find you don't have to *remind* yourself they are gone. You grow into your new chapter and come to terms with the fact you have to live the rest of your life without them. It's still difficult to live despite their absence."

Orinthia was taken aback by his honesty and transparency. She had barely known him for more than a few days, but he spoke to her like an equal. Like a friend. She was more surprised at how comfortable it felt to speak to him as well.

An intense pounding sounded on the outside of her door. Orinthia jumped up and dropped the photo on the ground. She bent to pick it up, but Thrutt was already at the door letting in whoever was on the other side. Quickly, she pushed the frame under the bed with her foot and jumped to her feet.

Kos dashed in. His coat was undone and looked like he ran the entire way from wherever he had been. He took a few deep breaths, then addressed Orinthia as he exhaled. "What happened?"

For the second time, she replayed the scene, explaining how she tried to fire her gun but it must have jammed.

"Thrutt said you have arm swords," Kos interrogated. "Why didn't you use those?"

She did not like his tone. It sounded more of an accusation than a question. "They are motion activated. I couldn't swing my arms enough to get them out." Orinthia crossed both her arms and flung them back to her side, revealing two silver blades.

Kos's hands pressed against his hips, and in one motion he had two gold plated pistols pointed at her chest.

"Stop," Thrutt shouted. His voice punched through Orinthia's body like a shock wave.

Kos and Orinthia looked at him. Strands of Orinthia's hair fell over her face, but she dared not move to fix it.

"Quartermaster, with all due respect, are you out of your mind? She was merely showing how her modification works." He then looked at Orinthia. "Nevertheless, you should not have done that. He is your superior. Do you two want to be exiled?"

Kos straightened his footing and let his pistols hang loose at his side. Orinthia retracted her blades and looked out the window.

"Now, if you will leave us, Rogue. We have a duel to prepare for," Thrutt said.

15

*T*he air around Orinthia was thick as she and Thrutt exited the lift onto the main deck. Her mind raced with thoughts. She had dueled as a Hunter. It was something she even enjoyed doing, but it was mostly ever other Hunters and no lives were at risk.

Thrutt led them through the familiar path to the observation deck. She looked up, hoping to be swept up and taken away to live among the countless stars. To be far away and not walking toward what could be her last moments, were she to make any mistakes.

Her fellow marauders murmured around her as she stepped into the center of the room. Her mod hummed, and though it picked up deceit, Orinthia could not make out what was said.

Thrutt tapped her elbow and signaled for her to focus.

It took a great deal of effort to break her eyes from the ceiling to face Captain Ahto standing on the second level she had fallen off. The rest of the crew stood on either side of him and watched. Orinthia's neck burned, and she felt small in the universe as she scanned the faces of alien multiple species she could not name.

"This must be a record." Ahto spoke so his voice carried to every ear. His head was held high and he looked down his nose at Orinthia. "Our newest member faces her first engagement on the first day of being part of our crew. I dare say most of you weren't even aware she was aboard our home."

Another stream of whispers moved through the crowd.

"Gunner Xyla fell defending this young human," Ahto continued. "It is now her duty to repay the act. What weapon will you use?"

Kos Rogue, who stood to the left of Ahto, pressed his hand to a button on part of the railing of the platform he and the others stood on. Below him, in front of Orinthia and Thrutt, the walls separated and exposed an arsenal ranging from blasters to golden hilted long swords.

Orinthia looked over her options, but none suited her better than the blades she already possessed. "I have my own, if that's okay."

Ahto waved his hand, palm up, for her to show him.

She looked at Thrutt who gave her a nod. With a deep breath, Orinthia took a step back, pressed one arm to her chest and tossed it to her side, leaving an arm normal in case she needed to use her hand. Light reflected off the metal. It was the only one of her two mods she chose for herself.

"What is the make of your sword?" Ahto asked.

"Martian steel," Orinthia answered.

The captain's eyes twitched to the blade, then at the corridor behind her. He lifted his voice again and shouted, "Bring in the defender."

Sounds of struggle came from the hall. Orinthia turned to see the man being dragged in. He squirmed and let profanities flow from his mouth. Orinthia quickly looked away.

"Human sailor," Ahto said once the man was set in his place beside Orinthia. "You stand guilty of killing a member of my crew, of my family. Your life now hangs in the balance."

The man grunted and continued to fight his restraints.

"As is our custom, we will allow you to walk out free *if* you can defeat the one Xyla sacrificed her life for."

He stopped resisting and stared at Orinthia. She did not meet his gaze, only she could feel his eyes boring into the side of her face. The bruised side he gave her. "The Interstellar Accords dictate I am a prisoner of war, and as such I have rights." He turned his attention back to Ahto.

Ahto grinned and stepped forward. Within a blink of an eye, he leaped from the balcony like an arrow and stood in front of the sailor. Not as Ahto the captain, but as Ahto the Irelad. His whole form changed.

Orinthia watched as all nine feet of the metal snake coiled around her opponent. The tail of which, as sharp as her own blades, pressed against his neck. The air in the room stilled and grew warm.

"The Interstellar Accords hold no sway on my ship," Ahto growled his words. His voice seemed out-of-place coming from the machine. In her mind, it belonged to a man. "Long have I been betrayed by those who command from the safety of their towers, playing their games, while my brothers and sisters die. The *Fera* does not recognize any Earth Confederate drivel."

Orinthia's father once told her about the Irelad—elite, fully autonomous, killing machines. They were created in the darkest days of the war, when the Earth Confederate was against the ropes, and their soldiers were being annihilated by the score. It was a last-ditch effort to quell the misuse of tech and modifications, but in doing so, they exhibited the most heinous misuse.

The EC, and all its scientists, created machines capable of memory, feelings, decision making, and emotion. They gave synthetic life. Then, when the war was won, the Earth Confederate left no place for Ireland to exist in the new, tech-stunted galaxy.

"The *Fera* runs on my orders," Ahto said. "Life demands a life." He unwrapped the man and slithered up the stairs to his spot. "Choose your weapon, human."

The man shivered for several seconds. His eyes were wide and looked far off, as if he was willing himself to be anywhere else. He must have realized hoping would not solve his problems and dashed forward. In three steps, he cleared the distance to the weapon wall and lifted the closest sword to him. He turned to face Orinthia, holding it out with both hands on the hilt.

Thrutt and the two marauders who dragged in the sailor stepped aside. It was the signal that the duel had begun.

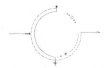

16

*T*he combatants walked in circles. When one would move, the other would go the opposite direction, like two magnets repelling each other. The young sailor's arms shook from the weight of the long sword, but he never lowered it.

Orinthia tucked in her elbows in, one arm as a blade and the other as normal and waited for him to strike first. Her heart pounded in her ears. The ache in her back dulled from the adrenaline coursing through her body.

Her rival stopped their dance and stood with legs apart. He drew in a deep breath and yelled as he lunged toward her.

As he came closer, Orinthia, too, inhaled but only to focus. She waited for him to close the gap. When he was a step away, she thrust her blade upward and deflected the charge.

The man stumbled but did not falter. He lifted the sword above his head and brought it down.

Again, Orinthia caught the blow with her blade.

He leaned into the attack and pressed his weight against their weapons.

She let him come closer, then lifted her leg, planted her foot into his stomach, and shoved back.

The crowd cheered. She had almost forgotten their audience.

The sailor flew backward onto his bottom but scrambled back to his feet.

They continued to swing and hit each other. Each blow vibrated her to her core. Her arms were reinforced to take the damage, but it did not dull the shock of the impact.

It was clear to her he had no experience in sword fighting. He used too much energy and over-extended his arms. His movements were stiff and slow, like trudging through thick mud. When she swung her blade, he would smack it away with the flat side of his sword.

Orinthia pressed on and swung rapidly. The thought of killing him had not fully formed in her mind. She only wanted to wear him out enough to make him give up. Maybe if he fought valiantly, Ahto would see the man's worth and let him go free. *If* they were as honorable as Kos claimed.

Her plan was working. The man's movements lagged, and it took longer between swings for him to attempt again. Sweat dripped from his forehead into his eyes, which he constantly wiped clear.

With a final swipe, Orinthia thrust her blade down, contacting his hand. She had not intended it to be so forceful, but her steel slid gracefully down the edge of his weapon.

The man yelled as his hand, still holding the sword, fell from his arm.

She looked up at Ahto, hoping the damage would suffice. Her chest heaved up and down as she caught her breath. He stared at her as if commanding her to continue. Orinthia did not break her eyes from his.

Another surge of whispers went around the deck as the crew watched the young woman stand her ground.

"Your duel is not over," Ahto said. "It ends when one of you is dead."

"I won't kill him," she said. "It is not my fault Xyla died. She did her duty. But so did this man." Orinthia pointed the tip of her blade to the sailor, cradling his nub as it bled into his shirt. "I was told this crew was honorable. Killing an unarmed man is the opposite of that."

Ahto glared at her, but she did not look away. The battle left her emboldened. When it was clear she would not comply, Ahto turned to Kos. "Finish it."

Kos' face was blank, but he followed his captain's orders. He jumped from the balcony and landed on the balls of his feet, crouching to absorb the impact. When he stood, a fire burned in his eyes. Not the fire of passion, but fire that destroyed. Like watching a building go up in flames from far away. He tossed off his coat.

Intricate tattoos covered the tight skin on his arms. On one arm was layer over layer of armor plating, like the ancient knights in Earth fairytales. The tattoo extended out of his capped sleeve down to his knuckles. The other arm had markings just as detailed. Gears, cogs, and pistons peeked through bracing. It was colored in a way that looked like the inner-working of a real machine. In the center of one of the crossbars, was an insignia on a shield.

"Pick up your sword," Kos said to the man. His voice was robotic and strained.

The man shook his head and mumbled pleas for his life.

"I said pick up your sword." Kos kicked the bloodied sword toward the man who continued to beg.

"You don't have to do this." Orinthia reached out to touch

him. His skin burned under her hand and the heat made her let go.

He did not seem to notice what she had done. He only continued barking orders at his prey.

The man curled into a ball and protected his head with his good hand, now soaked red.

Orinthia watched in horror as Kos touched his hip and drew the same pistol he had pointed at her. Her voice caught in her throat, and she could not yell out for him to stop. All she could do was stand witness to murder, one she had a part in.

The quartermaster lifted the golden blaster and aimed at the sailor. Pink mist sprayed out from behind his back as he fell to his side.

It took a second for her eyes to register what happened. No one in the room spoke. It was a haunting silence.

The moment caught up with her. Orinthia broke the stillness with a scream. "You are a liar! The speech you gave about honor and not being like other marauders is utter garbage. He surrendered and you killed him."

Kos turned on his heels and marched to her. The heat rolled off him as he shoved his face close to hers. His eyes continued to burn, and the fire was smoldering, threatening to engulf his entire existence. "I wouldn't have had to if you had done what you were told." He drew in air through his nose and pinched his lips together until they went white.

Orinthia stood her ground, though afraid he would fire upon her, too. At that moment, she realized the mistake she made. She was not marauder material. There was still too much Hunter in her, and as much as she tried to fight it, she could not kill in cold blood.

17

"*I* should have left you on that rock," Thrutt said when they were back in Orinthia's cabin. "It's obvious now you were going to be a headache."

Orinthia sat on her bed with her back against the wall and legs drawn up to her chest. Her boots laid limp on the floor and the rest of her marauder clothes were scattered around. She wanted nothing to do with them. They were replaced by a powder blue, over-sized sweater, and night shorts she had packed in the bag she brought from Earth. They smelled like her apartment.

She wanted to lash out at Thrutt, to tell him she already knew she was a worthless screw-up and to dump her off on the nearest planet. But the duel drained her.

"And what am I supposed to do?" Thrutt continued. "Ahto is going to have my head for this."

In the time she spent chasing marauders, she imagined they had an easy life. Flying across the known galaxies, having grand adventures, seeing new worlds. Maybe they did do all those things when they were not forcing fresh crew mates to execute young sailors. Maybe she would have done it, too, if she had tried a little harder to do as she was told.

The bed creaked and sagged a little as Thrutt sat on the edge. She had not realized he stopped talking. He patted her bare feet with his frigid hand. "I shouldn't have yelled at you."

Orinthia curled her toes so his hand slipped off, but she did not look at him.

"It's been a while since I've been responsible for someone else," he continued, unprompted. "I was more worried for you than I am angry at you."

Again, his candor and honesty caught her off guard. How was he able to worry about her? He did not even know her.

"You remind me of my youngest daughter," he answered her unspoken question. "Though I never found her in a drunken brawl inside a bar, she was full of fight. No one could tell her what to do. And when they tried, she did the opposite, even if it got her hurt. I think part of me hoped I could have relived those days through you. And for that, I'm sorry. You did not deserve for me to push those expectations on you."

"Why are you telling me this?" Orinthia whispered, afraid that if she spoke louder, she would either scream at him or cry, neither of which she had the energy for.

"I'm sure Ahto has already called a vote for us to be sent away," Thrutt answered. "Better to get it off my conscience before we are both locked in our cabins."

Orinthia pictured her and Thrutt on some dark planet in the middle of a solar system she never heard of. She wondered if she would go back to Earth or live out her days wherever they left her. Did she want to go back? Maybe she would find somewhere else, somewhere things grew. Where green meant life and the sound of water would trickle nearby.

Another image crossed her mind. A small loft high in the trees overlooking a stream. There was a balcony with dozens of plants soaking up the sunlight. And she would have a pet, whatever passed as a pet on the make-believe planet she was on.

Her daydream was shattered by a knock. It was not frantic like when Kos had gone in. This was deliberate and official.

Thrutt leaned over and pressed the button to open the doors.

Orinthia watched through the side of her eye as Ahto in his human form walked in. Her heart sank. Not only had she disobeyed orders, shouted at him in front of his crew, but she was also out of uniform. He was liable to shoot her out an air vent into the expanse for all her infractions.

"The crew voted," Ahto said. "They are more merciful than I am. Your brothers and sisters decided to give you a second chance."

Orinthia's head popped up. The movement made her dizzy.

"Your journey with us has only begun," Ahto continued. "We expect great things from you, Thia."

"We are staying?" she asked.

Ahto nodded.

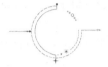

18

*D*espite her chaotic entry into marauding, the following two weeks were quiet. The deaths of Xyla and the EC sailor prompted Ahto to keep his ship on a low profile until things cooled down. Orinthia did not mind. She was still debating whether she wanted to continue with them, and the lack of action was a welcome lull.

None of the crew spoke to her about what happened, but she preferred to keep to herself when possible. Her only regular companion was Thrutt, who continued to mentor her. And though she technically won her fight, he wanted to make sure she was ready for the next one.

They spent hours a day dueling on the observation deck with swords, learning hand-to-hand combat, and practicing how to efficiently disarm her opponents. The training she had as a Hunter had to be unlearned. It was slow and predictable, just like the EC sailor's. Thrutt, though huge and made of actual stone, was graceful. He slashed through the air like a dancer. His movement was quick and steady, but also ready to dodge most of Orinthia's attacks.

The first time she hit him, she froze, afraid she wounded him. He only laughed. "There you go!" Then, as her face went pale, he said, "Your weapons can't hurt me. Stone doesn't bleed. It would take a lot more than you to damage me."

"Are your hands modified?" Orinthia asked. The question burned in her mind since she first saw him.

He nodded. "A gift from my former captain after the originals were blown off during my last tour. Turns out, cannons *are* something that can damage me."

"During our war or yours?"

"They were both my wars," Thrutt answered. He replaced the sword in the arsenal and closed the wall. "When my family was killed, I went to a dark place, content to fight and drown the pain away. Then a boy and his aunt dropped into my life. They set me right. When the Great Mod War began, the boy enlisted. His aunt begged me to keep him safe, so I joined along with him."

Orinthia waited for him to finish his tale. When he did not, she asked, "And? What happened to the boy?"

Thrutt smiled. "Don't worry. I kept my promise to his aunt. He is doing well today. Sometimes he needs reminding, but he is a good man."

Though she was glad to hear it, Orinthia kept her face still. Her heart ached with a pang of jealousy she could not place. Was she jealous of the boy or Thrutt? With a huff, she pushed the feeling away.

"Well," he said, putting his hands on his hips. Again, it seemed so human. "I may not look old, but I feel it. These sessions, though valuable for both of us, take a lot out of me. Perhaps tomorrow we'll have a break. Sound good?"

Orinthia nodded. She wanted to learn more, but her arms ached from constant use. Her joints ached. And it was probably only in her imagination, but she thought she felt one of her blades loosen.

THERE WAS nothing to do in her still-empty room. The *Fera* had not yet made port to sell the cargo taken from the EC ship. Because of that, Orinthia had neither been paid nor been able to purchase anything. She already read the three books she brought. And there was only so much scrolling the social nets on her PortTab she could stand.

The boredom morphed to hunger. Eating sounded better than staring at the same ceiling for another few hours until she fell asleep. Orinthia waited for the full-service portion of the dining to end before venturing out.

The mess hall was empty, save for a handful of crew members scattered throughout the room. Orinthia had shown up after hours often enough to decide these were the less social of the bunch. They kept to themselves, just like she did. It was a pleasant change from Thrutt who, though she found herself enjoying the time they spent together, never stopped talking.

With a tray in hand, Orinthia picked through the human section of food. Nothing stood out to her as overly desirable, so she opted for a water sphere and the last two protein cubes.

"Can I have one of those?" someone asked.

Orinthia looked over her shoulder to see Kos a foot behind her. He stared at her tray, avoiding her eyes. She could feel the unease come off him, as if it hurt to speak to her. It was the first time they had seen each other–let alone said anything–since her duel. The image of the dead man at Kos's feet crossed her mind.

She looked back at the cube, took it, and placed it back on the counter for him to take.

Kos stepped closer, his eyes still glued to the food. He was stiff. "Why are you here?"

His question confused her. "Because I'm hungry." She could not tell if her answer amused him or just made him angry.

He showed no emotion. "Why did you become a marauder?"

Orinthia thought about her answer. She did not even fully know why. If she were honest, she would have told him it was because she was impulsive and did things to spite her siblings. But the idea of explaining *that* was exhausting.

"Have you ever killed anyone?" he asked before she could give an answer to his previous question.

"No."

He let her answer hang in the air. Was it the right answer? Was it what he was looking for? "You're lucky, then. But maybe this isn't the right place for you."

"Ahto said I could stay," she defended herself. True, she thought the same thing, but she did not want anyone else to tell her that.

"The crew said you could stay," Kos said. "Ahto doesn't think you have what it takes."

Her mod hummed. "Ahto doesn't or you don't?"

Kos looked at her in the eye. The fire was gone. His eyes were dark and worn. "Ahto."

Again, her mod told her he was lying. "Thank you for the concern. I will do my best to show Ahto what I'm capable of. But maybe killing isn't everything. Maybe it isn't something I can come back from. I won't do it unless I absolutely have no other choice."

19

*T*ime moved oddly in space. Without the Sun, saying things like "day" and "night" felt awkward. It was relative. Since most of the crew served with the EC, they used Earth hours, but there were also no time zones in space. So, to ease some of the confusion, the crew created their own universal time aboard the *Fera*.

Once every twenty-four hours, the bosun sounded a whistle a single time through the speakers to signal the start of the day which was equal to six in the morning. Twelve hours into the "day" she did a double whistle for six in the afternoon. It took some getting used to, but having a set rotation was easier than guessing.

The morning whistle had blown half an hour a before a knock came on Orinthia's door. She was not yet awake and had to roll out of bed wrapped in her blanket to answer.

Thrutt stood on the other side, wide awake, and all smiles as usual.

"I thought we were taking a break," Orinthia mumbled, stepping out of the way to allow him entrance.

"Ahto is sending Kos and me on a run."

"What does that have to do with you being in my cabin this early?" Orinthia rubbed her eyes and sat on the edge of her bed, pulling the covers tight around herself.

"Wherever I go, you go, too. That's how this works."

The fog of sleep lifted slightly. "Where to?"

"Astro District 7," Thrutt answered. "We're going to see a broker on Rust Rock."

The name did not ring any bells for her, but she was interested, nonetheless. "A real other planet?" Her mind was alight with thought, casting the drowsiness off like the blanket she threw on the bed. Adora and Arsenio never let her off the ship when they did missions away, except to board enemy ships. Other than Earth, the only planet she had been on was a terraformed resort her family visited during one of the few holidays they took together.

"It's not that big of a deal." Thrutt held his hands out to settle her. "This isn't even one of the exciting ones. Just a basic metro hub, surrounded by a dome on an asteroid."

Orinthia did not care. It was off the ship and not Earth. "When do we leave?"

"Within the hour. Meet me in the bay so we can fit you for a spacewalk suit."

Before Orinthia could ask why, Thrutt turned and left. *Guess I'll find out when I get there*, she thought. She jumped from the bed, brushed her hair, and hurried to find clothes through the automatic closet. Orinthia had not been this excited since she was eight years old, when Uri passed his flying test. He and Orinthia took their father's hover car and cruised around the city, just the two of them. It was a wonderful memory in the sea of bad ones. There was no Adora, no Arsenio, and no Father. She did not have to spy or hide from anyone's rage.

The adult Uri came to her mind. He had to have discovered her missing already. Was he worried about her?

Her heart ached to talk to him again. Uri was the only one who did not hate her for her mod. He understood how she felt. The twins received a telepathic link to each other. Orinthia was turned into a lie detector. And Uri was a cyborg. The four reimagined children of one Desidario Anton.

The thought of her father made her flinch. Anger pricked at her chest. She hated that he still had so much power over her.

Orinthia clenched her hands and let the enmity flow through her until the weight of it sunk into the floor. Her arms tingled as she released the tension. She arched her back and shook off the bit of hate that lingered. Going through so many emotions at once left her weary, but she zipped up her boots and left those feelings on the ship.

THRUTT STOOD BESIDE KOS. They both looked up at a holographic map. As Orinthia moved closer, she saw the projection appeared out of Kos's palm.

Her heart skipped. In her grogginess, she missed the part where Thrutt said they would go with Kos. Their previous encounters were less than optimal, and she was not looking forward to spending any amount of time in close quarters with him.

He must have felt the same, for when Orinthia stopped in front of them, Kos fixed his eyes on the map like he was trying to transport to any one of the rocks in front of him.

True to form, though, Thrutt greeted her with a grin. "Just in time. Follow me."

Orinthia kept her eyes on the back of Thrutt's head as she walked by Kos. She was used to being around someone who felt hostile toward her, but it did not mean she liked it.

"Most of these are spoken for," Thrutt said when they stopped at a tall cabinet and unlatched the lock. "But I think we can find one that works. At least until you get your own."

The two of them rummaged through the grey suits. Some of them smelled like spoiled food. Thankfully, none of those fit her. After a dozen or so, she pulled one that was a little too loose around the middle, but the length was perfect.

"And here are your mag boots," Thrutt said, handing her a pair of white and black painted shoes. "They are an older model, so remember to charge them after every use or they'll be of no use when you need them."

Thrutt led her back to Kos, who had already recalled the map. He kept his back to them, facing the sloop.

Orinthia had not gotten a good look at *Freya* back on Earth. At first glance, she was just like any other transport vessel in the galaxies. Slender, with a squared off front for ramming through ice and other space debris. But standing that close, she could see the pieces that made *Freya* unique.

Tucked in behind the main thrusters were two retrofitted afterburners, poorly painted to match the rest of *Freya's* dusty hull. She was given mismatched parts, like miniature ion cannons, a hooked winch, and at the bow, two drills. It was rather familiar and resembled the android from the restaurant Thrutt had taken Orinthia to.

Through the side of her eye, she could see Kos's face as he stared at the ship. It was the first time she saw him happy. He smiled at *Freya* as if he found paradise.

20

"*A*re you sure you don't want to see how she works?" Thrutt asked Orinthia who had taken it upon herself to explore upper deck of the sloop. "She won't mind."

"It's not *Freya* I'm afraid of upsetting," she answered, sitting with her legs propped over two of the ten passenger seats. "I've successfully avoided Kos by staying out of his way. I'm not about to break that streak." It was not until they came out of light jump that she heard him speak at all.

"Approaching the Astro Districts," Kos announced.

"Go get your suit on," Thrutt instructed Orinthia. "We'll be there soon."

Orinthia walked past the cargo hold to the back of the upper deck and climbed down the ladder to the lower deck. To the left of the landing was the galley. She took a right down the narrow passage. The two sleeping quarters were on either side of the hallway, facing each other. Each had five bunks and a washroom.

She quickly dressed in her spacewalk suit. Her skin tingled and hands shook as she slipped the suit over her clothes. The cold of the material reached her through the fabric of her shirt and sent a shiver down her back. Her bare feet sunk into the mag boots she was given, and though they were not as comfortable as her own shoes, they fit better than the suit.

The walk back to the upper deck took slightly longer due to the added weight. Orinthia stomped her feet as she moved and almost fell over twice.

Thrutt was already laughing when she joined him. "Good thing this isn't a stealth mission."

Orinthia glared at him but kept her mouth shut. She trudged closer to look out a window. An orange orb grew in front of her. In the middle was a city encased in reflective glass.

Freya stopped before reaching the surface of the asteroid.

"Why did we stop?" Orinthia asked, moving back to Thrutt.

"You'll see when we get out there." He handed her a helmet and booster pack. "Put these on."

Kos stepped onto the upper deck as Orinthia clipped the last buckle for her pack. He too was wearing a helmet and booster but carried his boots in his hands. His feet slapped the floor until he stood beside Thrutt.

"Stay together as we head down," Kos said, putting on his boots. "We'll use *Freya's* winch to get us to the top of the dome. Follow it down until we reach it. It'll be thrusters from then on."

"Is there a front door or something?" Orinthia interrupted. "Won't someone notice we are coming in through their ceiling?"

Kos ignored her and continued, "Use the boosters sparingly. If anything goes wrong, we want to be able to get out in a hurry. Press the ignition for two seconds, then coast. Repeat until we're there. And touch nothing."

Orinthia froze as Kos looked at her for the first time. It was in surprise at first, then turned to offense that he singled her out. She opened her mouth to speak, but Thrutt spoke first.

"The dome has a hole," Thrutt said, drawing her attention to himself. "Some space junk broke through the shield and let in the rust from around the dome. Overnight, the city was infected, and everything that had been exposed to the virus turned to rust and crumbled."

"And I can't have it coming back to *Freya*." Kos finished his sentence with a hard period, leaving no room for questions or comments. Then he turned away and headed through the cargo space toward the exit.

Thrutt and Orinthia followed him. *Freya's* bay doors slid open, and Kos was the first to jump out. He grabbed hold of the controls on his booster pack and propelled himself to the winch. With his feet on the hull and a few tugs on the hook, he pulled it free and began his descent.

Orinthia stood at the opening and looked down. Her insides squeezed tight, and she felt dizzy. Every scenario ran through her mind. If she missed the cable, she would have to correct and use more of her thruster than planned. What if it malfunctioned after she jumped and she was left to drift away? How long would her air last? Would Thrutt come for her, or would Kos order him to leave her?

She wanted to be sick and took two steps back. There was pressure on the small of her back.

"You'll be okay," Thrutt said through the comms strapped to his head. He leaped from the ship and used his pack to guide him to the cable. But unlike Kos, who kept going lower, Thrutt looked up at Orinthia and waited. He waved a hand at her, signaling for her to follow.

Gathering all the strength she had, Orinthia willed herself

to step out. Once she was free of *Freya's* airlock, her body was weightless. But unlike when she left Earth, there was nothing holding her back. Instead of feeling frightened, she felt free. Like she *could* continue to glide through the expanse without restraint. Like she wished she could have done when she first stepped onto the observation deck.

"What are you doing? Grab hold of the winch cord," Kos said over the comm in her helmet. His stern voice tore her from her imagination, and she scrambled to take hold of the booster's controls.

Once she righted herself and gripped the steel cable, she followed her teammates down. It took ten minutes to complete the trip. Her arms were sore and her neck ached from tilting her head back to see where she was going.

An opening in the glass came into view as they neared the end of the line. It shocked her to see how small it was. Back on *Freya*, Orinthia had pictured a gaping hole, but up close it was not more than a few feet in diameter.

Kos continued down, using his booster as planned, until he was completely inside the dome. Orinthia followed close behind Thrutt. When she was through and able to see what was beneath her, her heart sank in disappointment.

21

*T*hrutt made promises of worlds beyond imagination when Orinthia first met him. Places she could not dare to dream of. But as she floated through the top of the dome, she saw what she had seen her whole life.

Desert.

The whole city below her was covered in dust. As far as she could see, there were no plants or living things at all. Only mounds of red.

"I've seen shipwrecks in better condition than this place," Orinthia said to Thrutt as they waited for Kos to finish connecting the winch's hook to the edge of the glass to keep it from drifting away.

Thrutt looked at her. "I told you it wasn't going to be glamorous."

Kos joined them and pointed to the only still-standing building in the hub. It was made completely of glass, therefore rust free. "Everyone lives in there now. The Glass Shard. That's where we have to go." He was the first to jet off, pressing down on the controls of his pack for a burst, then gliding through the air.

"It's the perfect spot for scoundrels like us to do business," Thrutt said as he and Orinthia followed. "Hunters don't come out here because it's a dead metro and not worth the risk to their ships."

"Whoever lives in there is trapped, right?" Orinthia noted the lack of ships and transport of any kind. "Does anyone ever leave?"

"Some did," Thrutt answered. "A few ships were able to get out before the virus infected their vessels. The rust ate everything within a few days. Those who couldn't leave fled to the safety of the building. They insulated it to contain their breathable air. Eventually, the rest will find a way in and finish it off."

Caged, Orinthia thought, *with no way out.*

No one else spoke until they neared the edge of the roof. They leaned down and made a sharp incline to land.

Four guards stood outside in all-black oxygen suits and held guns out at the trio.

"Stop!" One of the guards instructed. "Land on the ledge."

Orinthia could see a wide awning with an orange "X." She, Kos, and Thrutt did as they were told and powered down their boosters, hovering weightlessly above the marked location.

"What's your business?" A second guard asked, stepping closer to them.

"We're here to see a broker," Kos answered. His voice was steady and official, like he was made for this type of job.

"You all need to be scanned before entering," the first man said.

"For what?" Orinthia asked, feeling exposed in the dome's emptiness. Even the atmosphere had a red hue to it.

"No one is allowed inside until they can prove they are

uncontaminated. We can't risk allowing the rust in," the guard answered. He gripped his gun tighter.

"We didn't touch anything," she protested. "You had to have seen we haven't been lower than your roof."

"Thia," Thrutt said with force. "This is their home. They have the right to protect it."

Orinthia pinched her lips and squirmed in her suit. It was one thing getting a telling off on the ship, but another when strangers were watching.

The first two guards moved closer and stepped onto the ledge. A third stood a few paces behind with her gun still trained on them.

"Is that really necessary?" Orinthia asked.

"Shut up," the armed guard said. "If you move off that platform, it will be the last thing you do."

"I'm not going to move. Geez." Orinthia lifted her hand to make a gesture, but Thrutt grabbed her arm.

"Thia," he said, like scolding a child.

She huffed out through her nose. Having a gun pointed at her was less than ideal. Sure, it was part of being a marauder, but she would have liked to at least be able to point one back.

The three marauders were scanned one by one. The guards moved slowly, checking every crease of their suits. One stopped at Thrutt.

"Why aren't you wearing a helmet like the others?" he asked.

Thrutt knocked on his chest. "I'm stone. No lungs."

The man nodded, though he did not look happy about the answer. He stepped back and addressed the group. "All clear to enter. Take these." He handed them wristlets. "You're allowed one hour inside. These will tell you when your time is up. If we have to come for you, you will be banned and never allowed back in."

"Keep your helmets on," the woman guard said. "We have limited resources and they are not for sharing."

"To save time, maybe you can tell us which floor we can find Errol the information broker," Kos said.

"Do I look like a tour guide?" The second guard made a face. "Get inside or don't. But get off my roof."

Orinthia fought the urge to smack the guard. She did not want to risk a third tongue lashing from Thrutt.

Kos jumped from the roof, pushing off the edge of the platform with his feet. He cleared the distance to the door without using his booster. The other two did the same, and soon they were inside.

"Why did you let him talk to you like that?" Orinthia asked after the door closed behind them.

"It doesn't matter," Kos answered. "We got in. There is no use in burning a bridge we still need to cross." He crouched down and pressed a button on the side of his boots. "Make sure to turn on your mags. We can get around faster."

Orinthia tapped her own boots, and her feet sunk to the floor.

They walked down two flights of stairs before coming to a larger set of doors with the number "28" etched into the metal.

A bulky neon sign hung above the door. "Glass Shard Gallery."

22

*T*he inside of the gallery was the opposite of what they saw on the outside. Kos, Orinthia, and Thrutt stepped through the opening into a brightly colored conglomeration. Lights with colors that clashed with each other illuminated the walls. Orinthia understood what Thrutt meant about it being a metro hub. It was almost like they entered a shopping-mall-turned-city.

The center of the level was hollow with railing all around. Orinthia followed Kos and Thrutt and looked over the ledge to see through the opening. From there, all twenty-eight floors were visible, though the farther they were, the harder it was to make out what the signs read.

"We could turn off the mags and coast down," Orinthia suggested, straightening up and moving from the banister.

"That would be rude and unnecessary," Kos said. "We'll have to find someone who can help us."

Orinthia checked the timer on her wrist. There were only fifty minutes left, and each second they stood, there was wasted time. "We better start doing that, then. Because we're eating up our time just standing here."

She could hear Kos mumble through her comm, but he must have realized it because he quickly stopped and sighed loudly. Thrutt gave her a look like she was trying even *his* patience, which surprised her since she had hit him with a sword before, and that had not seemed to bother him at all.

They continued their way and walked down a few levels.

Chatter from around them seeped into Orinthia's helmet. Voices echoed through the shaft and mixed with the sounds of life. It was like being back on Earth. She had almost forgotten what crowds this large felt like and stayed close to Thrutt whenever they pushed through large groups. She was so attached to him that when he stopped, Orinthia crashed into his backside, making her cough a few times.

She looked around Thrutt and saw a young man, no older than a teenager, standing in front of Kos.

"Hey, pals," the boy said. "Whatcha looking for? Maybe ol' Arti can help. For a price."

Orinthia's head hummed when he spoke, but she kept quiet and listened to what he had to offer.

"Name the price," Kos said. "If I don't like it, then I'll take your hands instead."

Again, her mod sounded, which she found more interesting than the conman's lie.

"Look, my guy." Arti took a step away from Kos and put his hands behind his back. "No need to threaten me. I'll tell you whatever you want to know. Ninety credits."

"Ninety?" Kos reached into the pocket of his space suit, pulled out a dagger, and unsheathed it. "How about fifty and you keep your hands?"

"How about thirty and we call it a day?" Arti laughed nervously.

Kos covered the dagger and placed it back in his pocket. When he took his hand out again, he had three orange credit chips. "We need to find Errol the information broker."

"Sure, no problem." Arti's hand flew out in front of him. "Hand over the chips and I'll tell you where he is."

"Do you know exactly where he is?" Orinthia jumped out from behind Thrutt. He, Kos, and Arti stared at her.

Arti nodded.

"Use your words when speaking to a lady," Orinthia said, stepping closer. "I said, do you know exactly where Errol is?"

"Yes, jeez, back up." Arti held both his hands out to keep her away. "I know where he is."

Orinthia's mod was silent, so she continued with another question. "You're not going to take the money and trick us, right?"

"Ma'am, I'll have you know I am a gentleman." Arti pressed a palm to his chest and fluttered his eyelashes.

Orinthia stared back at him, her face as stony as Thrutt's.

"No. I won't trick you." He made a sound in his throat. "You two make a pair. Can't a guy earn a little money?"

Her mod stayed silent.

Kos blinked hard and shook his head. "Here. Now tell me where Errol is."

"He's on the sixth level." Arti snatched the credits out of Kos's hands. "Turn left out of the lifts and go two spaces down. His will be the smallest on the level. There isn't a sign above his place, but you'll know it's him when you see him."

Kos walked away.

"Thank you," Thrutt said to Arti for the first time, then followed his quartermaster.

Orinthia and the conman exchanged looks before she too left him alone.

When they were far enough away, Thrutt looked back at her and asked, "What was that about?"

She shrugged. "Seemed shifty. Some kid offering strangers tidbits for credits? Yeah, I wasn't buying it. Besides, Rogue was threatening to cut off his hands. I wanted in on the action, too."

Thrutt shook his head. "You two should give people the benefit of the doubt. Not everyone has a hidden agenda. I would have gladly given him the credits without putting fear into the heart of him."

"Are you sure you're a marauder?" Orinthia turned up her lip and wiggled her head.

Kos chuckled.

"I'm just saying that not every situation should be handled with a rocket-sledge," Thrutt said. "Some things need a scalpel. Diplomacy and tact wouldn't hurt."

Thrutt continued to lecture Kos and Orinthia on manners and negotiation etiquette until they reached the sixth-floor landing. Orinthia tuned him out and focused on their surroundings.

The walkway was dirty and used, piles of trash were scattered everywhere. It was darker, with fewer lights above the outlets. There were not as many people, either. Mostly humans, but she was not sure they could be called human anymore. They had dusty grey skin and dark, almost black, eyes. Their movements were slower than those on the upper levels. Decades of living with artificial light and dependance on mag boots changed them into something subhuman.

Maybe, she thought, *humans who left Earth long ago are no longer human, anyway.* She wondered if she would still be human if she never went back.

"This must be it," Kos said. He stopped in front of the place Arti described. It was inconspicuous, with no signage or evidence anyone lived there at all.

Though Orinthia suspected it was to keep away those who had no business with him.

23

"*Right* on time," a high, jingling voice said. "I'll be out in a moment."

Orinthia looked around but could not see who was talking. She squinted and tried to get her eyes to focus in the bright room. Light bounced through the haze, blurring her vision. It was as if someone smoked nonstop for hours on end. She could make out two couches and an over-stuffed, dark blue velvet lounge chair.

"Sorry," Kos said to the disembodied voice. "I don't think we are who you were expecting."

"Rubbish." The curtains in the back of the room flew open and a grey man stepped out.

Orinthia pinched her lips together. She had seen cyborgs before, even those who chose not to cover their bionics with artificial skin. But this was something different. Tubes and wires stuck out of the top of his head, which was completely bald, as overstuffed as the chair, and jiggled as he walked. He was no more than three feet tall and was lumpy under his clothes.

"I knew you'd be coming. And I know why," the man said.

"Are you Errol?" Kos asked.

"Yes, of course." The man hobbled closer to the group. "That is what my lease says, so that is who I must be."

"We've come with a question from Ahto, captain of the *Fera*."

Errol waved a hand like he was swatting Kos's statement out of the air. "I'll only speak to the human female."

"She doesn't know the question," Kos argued. Offense danced in his voice. "I'm Quartermaster. *I* was tasked with-
-."

Errol held up a hand. "I don't need to hear the question. I already know it. But I won't give the answer to anyone else but her."

Kos and Thrutt looked at Orinthia. She stared at Errol, avoiding the eyes of the others. Her skin warmed, and she flexed her fingers.

"Why her?" Thrutt asked. He had no judgement in his words. Only hesitation.

"Because I have what you want." Errol smiled. "So, I am at an advantage. If you are going to get the information, it has to be on my terms."

"We don't have time to argue," Orinthia spoke up. She pointed to the countdown. "Let me go so we can get out of here."

Kos grunted. "Ahto will not be happy."

Errol's grin grew. He stepped back through the curtain and held it aside for Orinthia to follow.

The back wall was lined with input ports, plugs, miniature screens, and slots for who-knows-what. There were two chairs in the center of the room facing each other. One had a stream of wires connected to it.

Errol waddled to that one and hoisted himself up. He stared at her with his bushy eyebrows up. "Have a seat."

"Why did you bring me back here?" Orinthia asked, stepping closer but not sitting. "I don't know what they're looking for."

He did not answer. Instead, he connected some wires and plugs into the ones in his head.

Orinthia wanted to turn away. It all felt very intrusive and private.

"I'm an information broker," he said, as if he heard the question hundreds of times before. "I trade information for information. But I am also a Sequencer."

Orinthia passed her weight from foot to foot, trying to find a comfortable way to stand. Her legs were tired from the mag boots and the chair looked more comfortable as the time went on.

"Every moment of every event is happening all at once," Errol continued, settling into his seat and closing his eyes. "It spans out for eternity. As a Sequencer, I can live those moments in an instant. I can take hundreds of paths and make dozens of choices in the time it takes to boil a cup of tea."

Orinthia rolled her eyes. "So, you're a fortune teller?"

"That sounds so antiquated. I analyze the sequences of events and determine the one most likely to be chosen. It is up to the receiver to follow those events or not. No future is guaranteed."

"Then why am I here?"

"Your path was more interesting than the others," he said, as if talking about why he chose the shirt he wore. "There are many crossroads before you."

Orinthia stayed quiet. Her pulse picked up and though the air in her suit was recycled, she felt like it was hard to breathe.

"You know I tell the truth."

She was about to ask him how he knew, but decided it was pointless. He was telling the truth.

"I'll give you a choice," Errol said, his eyes still closed. "You can ask me anything for yourself, or I can give you what you were sent for."

Orinthia looked at him with suspicion. "What information do you want in exchange?"

"None. I only want to know what path you'll take." Errol opened his eyes and looked at her. His dark eyes were alight. Colors swirled around the iris and shone brightly, like he was being powered by the plugs in his head.

Orinthia gasped and almost tripped over herself. It took a moment for her to regain composure. "I want the information we came for."

Errol grinned again. His teeth were brown and jagged. "Very well." He closed his eyes and leaned his head against the back of his seat. The room was silent.

Orinthia waited for the machines to whirr up, make a sound or do anything, but they did not.

"Take the data card from over there," he said.

Orinthia flinched.

"Insert it into any comm screen," Errol continued. "You'll find what you're looking for."

She did as she was told, eager to get out of his presence. With card in hand, Orinthia moved toward the door, but Errol spoke up and kept her from leaving.

"Do come back and let me know how it ends," he said.

Orinthia could hear the smile in his voice, though she dared not look back. She pushed her way through the curtain.

"Here." Orinthia shoved the card into Kos's hand.

He slipped it into his pocket and nodded.

Thrutt moved closer and looked her over. "You look upset. What happened?"

She shook her head, unsure of what to say. Nothing happened. But she could not shake the unease settling in her chest.

The alarm on her wrist made a sound. Time was almost up.

24

$\mathcal{T}$he wristlet alarms continued to sound, signaling five minutes until the trigger-happy guards from upstairs hunted them down. Five minutes to ride a lift twenty-eight levels up, run across a crowded deck, and race up two flights of stairs. Five minutes left.

"We aren't going to make it," Thrutt said.

Orinthia had an idea. Though she still felt weird about what happened a moment before, she grinned.

Kos rolled his eyes and shook his head, as if he could read her mind.

The three of them rushed out of Errol's hovel into the dark passage.

Orinthia bent down, deactivated her mag boots, and switched on her thrusters. As the boots lost grip, she kicked her legs out and jumped into the air toward the center of the gallery. When she was clear of the platforms, she jammed the ignition buttons on her pack and rocketed to the top.

It was a sensation she did not want to end. Flying weightless, nothing holding her back, up through the center of a building. She smiled, and though she still wore her spacesuit and helmet, in her mind her hair cascaded behind her, leaving a trail of silver as she flew.

Her fantasy ended when she reached the top, however.

Two of the guards were already leaning over, their mouths wide open, watching the strangers jet through their home.

"What do you think you're doing?" One of them yelled as Orinthia, Kos, and Thrutt hovered on the other side of the railing. "You can't use thrusters in here."

Orinthia pushed herself closer and mag locked her boots again as she landed beside the men. "We made it on time." She held out her watch. They still had two minutes left.

The guard set his jaw tight and glared at her. "Get out before I decide to permanently remove you."

Thrutt mumbled apologies as they passed, but Kos and Orinthia said nothing.

BACK ON *FREYA*, Orinthia sat on a seat with her feet propped on an armrest. As she looked out the window and watched the dusty rock shrink from view, she could not help but feel proud.

Her pride was quickly challenged by Kos who stormed in from below deck.

"That was reckless," he shouted. "You had orders to follow. I explicitly said we were not to do that."

"No, you said it was unnecessary at the time." Orinthia picked at her nails. "I'd like to remind you we had a deadline and we were going to miss it. I call that pretty necessary."

"There would have been another way. The right way." Kos was right in front of her.

Orinthia stood up. If he wanted to get in her face, she

would make it easy and get back into his. "I'm not a soldier, and you are not my captain. We are marauders. There shouldn't be *rules*. All I see is a soldier who is still playing war and can't move on."

"Thia, that is enough," Thrutt shouted. His voice filled the level and reverberated through her. "He is not only your superior and highest authority off the *Fera*, but also a veteran who would have laid his life down if asked to. We did not become marauders for the benefits and glamor. The people we fought for turned their back on us and made no place for us to return to. If you cannot respect his position, respect his sacrifice."

Orinthia backed down, though her pulse continued to thrum through her veins. She looked at Thrutt. "I have one overbearing father. I don't need another one."

Thrutt shrunk down like he was deflating. His face went blank. "You're right. You don't need a father." Without saying anything else, he turned and left down the ladder.

Kos shot her a look that had it been tangible, would have cut her right to the core. He took off after his friend.

The shift in atmosphere almost knocked the wind out of Orinthia. She wanted to reach out and pull her words back. Thrutt had been the only one who cared about her since she joined. True, she did not need a father, but she did need a friend. And she chased her only one away.

Orinthia sat down in her seat again and placed her head in her hands. She filled her mouth with air and slowly pushed it out. The surrounding area seemed to expand as the weight of her words settled. Every moment of the last few hours rushed through her head. It made her dizzy.

Then, the moments faded into junctures of her past.

Her life flowed from one chaotic mess to the next, never stopping long enough for her to catch her breath. The universe spun around her, dragging her down like a drain.

Expectations of who others wanted her to be came crashing down and she tried to claw her way back up.

The swirling stopped and she was looking down on her life as if through a glass ceiling. Desidario stood in front of his two middle children, scolding them, while little Orinthia watched from behind him. He left the room, and the three children were alone. The twins tackled her as she tried to run after him. Adora sat on top of Orinthia's chest and shoved strips of fabric into her ears. Orinthia screamed for help, but Arsenio cupped his hands over her mouth.

Like the flash of a bulb, the scene changed, and teenage Orinthia stood alone before her father. He was yelling, though silently through the glass. She yelled back. Desidario raised a hand and smacked her across the face, knocking her to the ground.

The Orinthia watching from above flinched but could not look away. It was the first time her father discovered she lied to him, but it would not be the last time she would try. It was then she realized she could never escape her family's rage.

Another flash and she was standing on the ledge of her apartment's roof, looking over the city. The wind whipped her hair around her face. Her heart pounded in her chest and ached like it was physically breaking. Tears streamed down her cheeks in waves. She could hardly draw in air.

Uri stepped into view. He took her hand and yanked her back from the ledge. His arms cradled her as she sobbed into his shirt.

The world lurched around her again, and she opened her eyes. Orinthia lay on the cold floor inside *Freya*, gasping for air as if she had never breathed before. Her body shook like she was freezing, though she could feel sweat prickle her skin. She did not know what happened, but she wanted to never experience it again.

$\mathcal{D}$ ishes clanged together as Orinthia rummaged through the galley's supplies. Her panicked episode left her mouth dry and stomach hungry. Its food was less stocked than she would have liked, but she found something to satisfy her emptiness. Orinthia carried her armful of Earth fruits and bagged treats to one of the tables and sat with her back against the wall and crossed her legs.

There was still tension lodged in her spine, but she hoped eating would help ease some of it. Endorphins rushed through her brain with each bite. Orinthia was at peace with herself again, at least for a while.

Once she calmed down and could think clearly, there was only one thing left to do. The thought of it almost made her stomach bring up its undigested contents. She knew what she had to do, but she did not know how to say it.

Growing up, she was forced to apologize for everything. Forced by her siblings to apologize to them for tattling, hoping their retaliation would be avoided. Forced to apologize to her father for lying to him, to avoid the beating from him. But she did not know how to be sincere.

Orinthia slid off her seat and stood on wobbly legs. She trudged her way to the quarters in hopes of finding Thrutt alone. Her feet made no sound since she had yet to put her shoes back on after taking off her spacesuit. She imagined herself a ghost moving through the corridor and tried to detach herself from the moment.

But when she saw Thrutt, the moment crashed into her, and she was very much in it.

Thrutt sat on a bottom bunk, facing away from the door. His head hung low, not moving.

Orinthia cleared her throat to catch his attention. Her legs almost gave out when he glanced at her.

"What?" he asked.

She swallowed the saliva that pooled inside her mouth before speaking. "Can I talk to you?"

"I'm busy," Thrutt said, looking away from her again.

Orinthia did not need her mod to tell her he was lying. She stepped in and stood a few paces behind him. Seeing his face would be too hard, but she could muster the strength to speak to his back. "I can't take back what I said, but I know I shouldn't have said it."

Thrutt sat quietly.

"I have spent my whole life on the defensive," she continued. "If you knew what my family was like, you would understand. I felt attacked and lashed out."

Thrutt turned around and looked at her in eye. He shook his head as he spoke. "Correcting you is not an attack. Hurting others because you are hurt does not excuse poor behavior. Take ownership of your mistakes and deal with them without passing the blame on others. Now, try apologizing again."

Orinthia pulled her head back. *Is he giving me advice on how to say sorry?* She took a deep breath. Her stomach knotted and churned. "I'm sorry you were hurt by…"

"No. Again," Thrutt interrupted her.

Frustration pricked at her eyes. Orinthia blinked away tears. "I don't know how."

"Yes, you do. Try again." Thrutt did not shout. He did not look at her with disdain. It was as if he were coaching a child, teaching her a skill she needed to master.

Try as she might, the tears flowed from her eyes. Orinthia stood in the middle of the room, her chest tight. "I'm sorry I hurt you," she whispered.

Thrutt stood up and put an arm around her shoulders.

Orinthia wanted to move away, to run away. To be anywhere but standing where she was.

"Now apologize to yourself," he gently said. "You've held onto this pain for too long. Whatever happened to you is behind you. Choose to move on and be better because of your past, not bitter. Only you can decide how to handle the afflictions in your life."

Orinthia crumpled to the floor under the weight of his words. She sobbed and heaved into her hands. Her heart ached like she would never be happy again. Every cry was loud, but after several minutes on the ground, the weight lifted. She could breathe more easily and though her pain was still there, it hurt less.

Thrutt stood over her in silence. Not in awkward silence as if he witnessed her have a meltdown, but almost in reverence, allowing her to grieve freely. Like he guarded the chamber of her sorrow while she was vulnerable and exposed.

Orinthia wiped her eyes on her sleeve and looked at the ground. "Well, that was embarrassing."

"Admitting you are wrong is uncomfortable and frightening," Thrutt said. "But growth is not embarrassing."

Still not looking up, she thought about the words she shouted at Kos. "I'm not done apologizing, am I?"

"No, but I don't think he's ready to hear it. To him, he was never 'playing war.' It was all he wanted to do. He was never prouder of himself than when he enlisted with the Earth Confederate Navy. Then they took his service, used him as a weapon, and tossed him aside when they were done."

Thrutt's story of the boy crossed Orinthia's mind. "He and his aunt are the ones who saved you, weren't they?" She drew the courage to look up at him.

He nodded. "Rogue's mother died when he was young. Like many before the war, she grew addicted to modifications and started buying them secondhand. Her body could only handle so much, and eventually, it gave out. His father was also a sailor with the EC in the early days of the Great Mod War. When he went missing, the Navy assumed he deserted and came looking for him."

"They hounded Rogue's aunt, who to her dying day swore she had no idea where he went. The EC put a hold on all her accounts to ensure she was not helping him. Enlisted sailors owe the Navy for their mods. Most of the time it is paid off with time served, but if a sailor is injured or missing and cannot pay off the debt, it falls to the family to pay it. She had to care for Rogue and could not go in his father's place. Then, because of the hold on her accounts, she could not keep up with the bills."

Thrutt paused and looked in the direction of the cockpit. "Eventually they lost everything and were put on the street."

"How did you meet them?" Orinthia listened intently to his story, her anger rising for little Kos and his family.

"Earth was the farthest I could get away from my home planet. One day, I was passed out in an alley when the little runt tried to steal my last credit chip. He was not smooth and woke me up. His little face was full of terror and grime. Even through my haze, I could see he needed help. I gave him the chip, no questions asked. An hour later, his aunt had him by the arm, scolding him for what he had done. She made him return the credit. I offered to split a meal with them. It took some time, but eventually I sobered up and we all took care of each other."

Orinthia tried to picture Kos as a child. She placed the dirty little boy beside the grown proper man. They did not fit together, and she had a hard time believing they were the same person. "Why was he so eager to join if they treated his family so poorly?"

Thrutt shook his head. "That is his story to tell. The rest was just so you could understand who he was before."

he rest of the flight was quiet. All the excitement and tears left Orinthia drained, and she fell asleep on a bunk. Her dreams were jumbled. Both her and Kos' childhoods meshed inside her head. They sat on the grass in her mother's cemetery, laughing and playing together. Each understood how the other felt about losing a parent. She had a friend.

When her father came for her, she cried and tried to run. Little Kos stood up to Desidario and tried to keep him away. The sunny day turned dark as he moved toward the children. They shrunk back and looked for a place to hide. He moved closer and closer until he froze with his hands out, two steps in front of them. His shirt filled with red.

The children screamed inside Orinthia's dream, and her eyes flew open.

She was back inside *Freya's* cabin. A dim light above her bunk illuminated the space directly around her. No one else was in the room and she vaguely remembered Thrutt saying he was going somewhere. Orinthia let her head sink into the pillow and steadied herself. The memory of the dream faded like a puff of smoke, but she could not shake the fear.

The sloop shook and rocked, causing Orinthia to get out of bed to investigate. Through the window of the galley, she could see *Freya* dock inside the *Fera*. Ahto was already waiting inside the bay. Orinthia assumed Kos must have transmitted their approach.

She rushed out of the quarters, climbed the ladder, and put her shoes back on before they completed their landing sequence. With Kos still upset with her, she did not want to add her attire to the ammunition.

Freya's doors hissed as the airlock disengaged and opened. Orinthia made for the exit but was blocked by Ahto climbing aboard.

"Captain," Orinthia said, darting her eyes away from him and looking toward the opening. She placed her hands behind her back to keep them from shaking.

Ahto dipped his head at her. "Welcome back, Thia. Where is your pilot?"

As if summoned, Kos Rogue entered from below deck. He looked straight at Ahto. "I have your data chip, Captain. Errol said to place it in any comm screen to read it."

"What are we waiting for?" Ahto clapped his hands together. "Let's go to the control room and see what we have."

Orinthia watched as her captain and quartermaster descended the ladder. She once again made to leave, but Ahto called for her from below. "You are not dismissed until we view the information. Join us down here."

She hung her head back and sighed, turned on her heel, and crept to the cockpit.

Ahto and Kos were already looking at the screen when she joined them. Thrutt leaned against the corridor wall outside the door with his arms crossed. He looked at Orinthia and gave a side smile.

"All it says it 'He's on Elendoras'," Kos said.

"That's it?" Frustration oozed from his words. He pounded the screen repeatedly.

"What did I miss?" Orinthia leaned in and asked Thrutt.

"There is practically nothing on the chip," he answered. "They've already checked it twice."

"I'm guessing this was not the answer he was looking for," she said.

"Elendoras doesn't exist," Thrutt said. "Or not anymore. It's a dead planet. More than dead, blown up. The EC had a base there, and two years into the war, the Mod Bleyers wiped it out of the stars."

Orinthia could not recall that fact, but she also tuned out most things about the war. It was her father's world and she wanted nothing to do with it. She watched the two men continue to take out and reinsert the chip.

Ahto shook. His pale skin shimmered as he transformed into his snake form. He grew three feet and filled the room with his body.

Thrutt grabbed Orinthia's arm and they stepped back.

"Who is he looking for?" Orinthia asked Thrutt.

"My creator," Ahto shouted, turning on her. He towered over her. "The one who made me this way."

She impulsively took a step away and crossed her arms. With her back against the wall, and Ahto as close as he was, she could not activate her blades.

"No doubt you've wondered why I am alive when all my kin have vanished." Ahto forced his tail behind her and pulled her closer. He curled around her until they were face to face. If he had breath, she would have felt it on her skin.

Orinthia tried to close her eyes, to imagine herself somewhere else, like under the bed where she found her mother's picture. But he squeezed tighter and did not let her focus on anything but him.

"I have, too," Ahto said. "Years have I searched for answers. Countless warships, half a dozen generals, data broker after data broker. Until two years ago. We captured an EC cruiser. Just my luck, they happened to be transporting servers with encrypted war data to Congress. My analyst dug through every code until she found my ID number listed beside a name."

Ahto uncoiled himself and moved away, shifting back into his human form. "Desidario Anton," he said, straightening his coat as if about to be inspected.

Orinthia's throat sealed up, preventing any sound she would have made from escaping. She swallowed hard and tried her best to stay still.

"He designed me, and only me," Ahto continued. "Only he and his assistant knew I differed from the others. But Anton went missing shortly after we discovered this information. His assistant spoke out about the matter, in fear I had something to do with it."

"And he is who we wanted Errol to find?" Orinthia kept her voice steady.

Ahto nodded. "Elendoras is gone, therefore Errol must have lied."

"He didn't," she said without thinking. "At least he didn't seem like it."

The captain cut his eyes at her. "What do you mean, 'seem'?"

Kos spoke up. "Errol refused to give me the data. He only wanted her."

Ahto whipped his head back and forth between Orinthia and Kos. "You let him cheat me out of my information? Of course he wanted her. She can be fooled. You, Kos Rogue, were to get it. No one else."

Kos opened his mouth to speak, but Orinthia interrupted him. "He didn't have a choice. Errol refused. Kos didn't mean to make you upset. I must have gotten the wrong information."

Ahto faced her, though he stayed in his human form, and grabbed her by the shoulders, slamming her into the wall.

Orinthia squeezed her eyes shut and tried to cover her face. Ahto pinned her against the wall and she could not move her arms.

"You have failed me twice, then. All three of you will go back and get the correct information."

Orinthia's heart was in her throat. She wanted to shove him away, but she could not.

"Get my information, now." Ahto released her and disappeared up the ladder.

27

*O*nce again, Orinthia sat alone in the galley, staring at the wall. Even if *Freya's* windows were not closed, she would have seen nothing, anyway. Her mind raced in a hundred different directions. No thought lasted for longer than a minute before being overtaken by another.

She had known Desidario designed weapons for the war. It's what allowed him access to the mods he used to reimagine his children after civilian use of military tech was banned. Though she never knew what he worked on, the pieces fell into place in her mind. Her father told her about the Irelad. He told her how they worked and what they did. But as a young girl, she did not understand why. Irelad were not the only war tech he spoke of, so to her, they were just another subject she was too young to care about.

Orinthia's head spun, and she wanted to be sick. How much did Ahto know about Desidario? How much had the twins known about him? Did they know the EC wanted Ahto for Desidario's disappearance?

"Are you okay?" Thrutt asked, putting a hand on her shoulder.

Orinthia jumped out of her seat, unaware he walked in. "Yeah," she lied after his question worked its way through her congested thoughts.

"Ahto can be aggressive," he said.

Her mind searched for what he meant, then remembered the scene from the corridor. Orinthia tried to block it out again, but it was too late. It flowed through with the rest of her thoughts.

"I won't speak badly about my captain," he said. "But I will say I can't always agree with his approach."

Orinthia nodded, lost in her head again.

"Are you sure you're okay? I can have Kos scan you if you hit your head."

"I'll be fine," she said weakly. "It's been a long day."

Thrutt bobbed his head and turned to leave.

Orinthia spoke up. "Has Ahto found anything else about Anton?" she asked, testing the waters.

"Only that he was a scientist with the Earth Confederate war efforts," he answered. "Though Ahto believes he may have been playing both sides."

The air in the room went cold. Her father was a traitor? He was a horrible man, but even so, she could not imagine him committing treason.

"Maybe you should drink something," Thrutt suggested. "You're looking pale."

Orinthia wanted to keep asking questions but kept her words behind her teeth. She had to work things over more before she could decide the right ones to ask.

ORINTHIA'S LEGS were stiff when Kos announced they were almost to Rust Rock again. She stood up from her stool in the galley, stretched, and went to the quarters to put on her spacesuit.

The journey back through the dome was quiet. Orinthia did not know what to say to keep them from going back. She knew Errol had told the truth when he said he would give her the information Ahto asked for. Going back was pointless.

Then a thought hit her. She could ask him for information for herself. He offered it once, and maybe she could trade some of the Hunters' secrets for what she wanted to know. Would it be enough? What would she ask? She felt sick again and swallowed it down to avoid making a mess inside her helmet.

The same four guards were on the roof of the Glass Shard, watching as the marauders landed on the platform again.

"You gotta be kidding," the woman said. "After a stunt like that, you come back expecting to be let in again?"

Orinthia pinched her lips together. There was too much to lose for her to fly off the handle.

"I offer you our sincerest apologies," Kos said, dipping at the waist. "If you allow us entry one more time, it will not happen again. I swear."

The guards exchanged looks, then raised their guns. "How about you just fly back to wherever you came from? We don't need you causing any more trouble."

"We can pay you one hundred credits for entry," Kos offered.

The man squinted.

"Each," Orinthia said. "You'll each get a hundred credits." She glanced at Kos and made an 'oops' face. They needed to get in at any cost.

"Deal," the second guard said.

Kos grumbl"ed as he pulled a cloth bag from his suit's pocket. He tossed the guards two red chips each.

The woman nodded to the third guard, who scanned them. When they were cleared, she gave them their timers.

"Thirty minutes?" Orinthia panicked. "We had an hour last time."

"Call it a penalty for flying your jet packs through my building," the third guard said with a shrug. "You better get going."

Orinthia wanted to push him off the side of the building, but gripped her fists tight and held her arms close to her side. There was not enough time and they were going to have to run.

The three marauders pushed past the men and shot into the building, only stopping to engage their mag boots. As fast as they could, they maneuvered through the crowd toward the lift. Twenty-two levels took ten minutes to get through. Swarms of people exited and entered at every stop.

Orinthia wanted to scream. She wanted to shout that the lift was unavailable so they could get down faster. She bounced on the balls of her feet, though it was difficult to do so with them stuck to the floor.

"We'll get there, don't worry," Thrutt said to her.

The lift doors opened on the tenth floor and the rest of the people got off. Orinthia slammed her hand against the number "6" and did not let go until they opened on her level. She was the first one out, dashing for Errol's dark door.

Smoke still hung in the air, and though she felt like a lot had happened since they were last there, she realized only a few hours had passed. Not much would have changed, if anything at all.

Except Errol sat on the overstuffed lounge seat, grinning from ear to ear. "Right on time," he said for a second time.

"*a*hto is not pleased with the information he received," Errol said. It was not a question. He puffed out a ring of smoke and leaned back into the velvet chair.

"He believes you to be a liar," Kos said.

"Your captain can believe whatever he likes, but it does not change the facts." Errol did not flinch or move. It was as if he had no worries that three marauders stood in front of him.

"This will not end well for you," Kos threatened. "Give us what we came for."

Orinthia stiffened. Would he really kill Errol over this? What about the question she had for him? How would she be able to ask it in the time they had without the others knowing?

"I already did that," Errol said, sending more circles into the air.

Kos pulled the dagger from his pocket and stood with his feet apart, the dagger gripped in his hand and pointed at Errol.

Orinthia looked up at Kos. His face looked like it did

when he killed the sailor; distant, like someone else controlled him. As if he was doing the act out of pure duty to his captain and took no pleasure in it.

"Rogue," Orinthia whispered. It was the first time she spoke to him since their shouting match.

He did not look at her.

"Kos, don't," she said. "He is telling the truth."

"You can't know that, Thia," Kos said through clenched teeth. "He is a liar and a scam."

"But I do." The words squeaked out of her mouth. "I know he is telling the truth." Orinthia stepped between Kos and Errol with her arms spread wide.

"I knew you couldn't make it as one of us." Kos looked at her. "You continue to live in this fantasy where you can challenge orders from your captain. And now you defy *me* as I once again have to fix a problem you created."

Orinthia stood with her chin up, emboldened by the anger brought on by his accusation. "I can prove it. Tell me anything. I'll tell you if it is a lie or a truth."

Kos scoffed. "What?"

Orinthia could see the confusion on his face, but he quickly masked it with darkness again. She tried to find the little boy Thrutt spoke of. The one who dreamed of being a soldier. "Just do it. It's the only way I can show you."

Kos stood silently with his dagger unmoved.

"My youngest daughter's name was Amoly," Thrutt said.

Orinthia nodded. "That's true."

"The last time I saw my wife, she wore a blue dress and we watched the three suns set," Thrutt said again.

"Yes, that's true."

"The first ship I ever served on was ECS *Lotus*," Kos said with a low voice.

The bees danced around inside the jar in Orinthia's head.

"That's a lie. Now my turn." She drew in a breath. "My blades aren't the only mod I have. Each of my siblings were given unique 'gifts,' as my father called them. Mine is the ability to know when someone is lying."

"That's ridiculous," Kos said, waving for her to move.

"My father was not a good man." Orinthia pressed on, ignoring his comment. Her anger built up and filled her chest. "He used me to keep my older sister and brothers in line. He hit me when I refused to use my mod for his gain."

"Why didn't you tell us when you joined?" Kos asked, his dagger dipping.

Orinthia's eyes twitched to the blade, then back up. "You, of all people, should know the answer to that. I didn't want to be treated like property anymore. Always doing the will of others. I wanted my freedom and to live where no one knew about it."

Kos looked over her head toward Errol. "What're you so pleased about?"

Orinthia turned to face Errol as well.

He chuckled to himself. "This is exactly why I gave her the information and not you."

"You knew I would have to tell them," Orinthia said. "That I would have to expose myself in order to save you."

"That's not all," Errol said in a sing-song voice. "You're forgetting to tell them who your dear papa is."

Orinthia wished she had let Kos kill him. "Shut up."

"What is he talking about?" Thrutt asked. His words were soft and out of place in the tense atmosphere.

Orinthia glared at Errol before turning to face her companions. "I want to be clear that I did not know who or what Ahto was looking for when we were sent here."

"Go on," Errol coaxed.

Orinthia closed her eyes for a moment and blew air out of

her nose. "The man who made Ahto is the same man who made me this way." She pointed to her head. "Desidario is my father."

Errol erupted in laughter behind her.

She spun around and screamed, "Shut up, you creepy little monster! Why are you doing this?"

"Because it is fun," he said. "You were at so many crossroads, I could not clearly see which one you would take. Would you tell them? Would you not? Will you go after him? And I can tell you, this is my favorite timeline. It's rare I get to be part of the paths I sequence."

"You're sick," Kos said. "What gives you the right to play with people's lives?"

The alarms on their watches rang out. Its sound thrust Orinthia back into reality. She had forgotten all about their time restraints. "Where is he?" she asked Errol. "Tell me where he is."

"I've already done that." He puffed out another smoke ring.

"But that planet doesn't exist. He can't be there." Orinthia's mod was silent. He was not lying to her, but she felt like he had to be.

"It's time to go," Thrutt said.

"This is just the beginning," Errol said. "Everything is about to change for the three of you. Be sure to pick the right side."

Orinthia lunged for him with her hands out, ready to strangle the life out of him. But two diamond hands caught her midair and hoisted her back. She screamed obscenities and kicked as Thrutt carried her away. He did not let her go until they were outside the lift.

The doors opened on each floor again, passengers filed in at every level. They threw looks at the three spacesuit-clad strangers with alarms blaring. The sound only grew louder as their time reached the end.

When the lift stopped on the twenty-eighth level, the four roof guards met Kos, Orinthia, and Thrutt. All had their rifles aimed at center mass.

a crowd of onlookers formed around the standoff. Hushed voices passed between the people in waves. No one moved.

Orinthia wracked her brain trying to figure out a way she could use her blades without damaging her suit or getting shot in the process. She ran scenarios in her mind, but none of them ended with them alive. So, she had to wait to hear what the guards said.

"You're in violation of protocol 594," the woman guard shouted. "No outsider is lawfully allowed inside the Glass Shard after their allotted time has expired. Surrender your wristlets and prepare to be escorted out of the building."

Kos, Orinthia, and Thrutt slipped off their watches and held them out.

"Drop them and put your hands up," another guard shouted. "If any of you try to pull another stunt, I will shoot you."

That's a little extreme, Orinthia thought, but she kept it to herself.

The marauders marched in a line to the exit and up the

stairs. They were almost to the top when the door behind them opened.

"The broker is dead," someone shouted.

Orinthia's mod hummed, and she looked down. Arti stood at the base of the steps, panting.

"They killed him," Arti said.

Again, Orinthia's mod hummed. She did not wait to give a defense or argue. With all the force she could find, she ran up the last few steps and out the door. There were no guards on the roof, and it was empty.

Kos and Thrutt were on her heels. They all ran to the platform, but there was no time to turn off their mag boots.

With her pulse pounding in her ears, Orinthia took hold of her comrades and pulled them forward with her as she leaped from the building. As they drifted away, she let go of their arms and activated her booster pack. "Punch it," she shouted into her mic.

They shot upward as blaster fire flew past their heads.

Orinthia stole a look back. Two of the guards had donned their own packs and gave chase. She swerved as one fired a shot directly at her.

A hail of blaster bullets followed them. Kos, Thrutt, and Orinthia weaved in all directions to avoid getting hit.

"We're almost there," Kos shouted. "Don't stop until we are back on *Freya*."

The opening in the dome grew larger as they approached. Orinthia could see stars through the crack. She willed herself to move faster.

A burning pain ripped through her side. The oxygen was sucked out of her suit. She fought to breathe and felt faint. Her grip loosened on the controls. Seconds passed before the auto repair kicked in, and the suit patched the hole.

Orinthia gasped and filled her lungs with air again, but the burning did not stop. She let a hand come off one of the stabilizers and pressed it to the spot. When she pulled her hand back, there was blood on her glove. Warm liquid trickled down her back inside her suit, but she pressed on, fighting through the pain.

"Are you hit?" Kos asked. There was panic in his voice.

"I'm fine," she said through gritted teeth. They were still in a race to the ship, and there was no time to stop. She would have to make it to safety.

Thrutt was the first out of the dome, followed by Kos, Orinthia, and the two guards.

The pain made Orinthia weak. She could hardly press down on the thrusters and slowed down to a coast with the guards close on her tail.

Kos looked back, cursed, and turned his body toward her. "Grab my hand."

Orinthia reached out, but the stretch pulled at the wound and she coiled back.

Kos grunted. He swung around her, grabbed her arm, and dragged her up to the ship.

When they reached *Freya*, Thrutt had already disconnected the cable from the winch with the emergency lever and tossed it, so it floated out of the way.

Kos cut his thrusters as soon as they entered the airlock, and he and Orinthia crashed to the deck, skidding across the ground.

"*Freya*, emergency jump, now!" he shouted and kicked a bar for the bay doors to seal.

The two guards appeared for a blink as the doors snapped shut.

Thrutt tossed his pack off, took hold of Orinthia, and lifted her out of the hold. He held her like a baby, with one arm cradled under her as he climbed down the ladder and placed her on a bed.

Kos ran behind him. He ripped off his helmet, and Orinthia could hear it crash against the wall somewhere. He pressed two fingers to his temple and activated his visor.

"We need to get her back to the *Fera*," Kos said. "Her heart rate is elevated and she's losing a lot of blood."

"The blue stuff," Orinthia muttered to Thrutt. "Like my arm."

Thrutt shook his head. "That's just for minor injuries. You're seriously hurt."

Orinthia nodded. Her eyelids dipped, and it grew harder to keep them open with each blink.

"No, stay here." Kos shook her. "You're going to be fine."

"Liar," she mumbled.

He slammed his fist on her chest. The suit suctioned tight against her body. Orinthia hissed in pain. Without saying another word, he ran from the room.

Orinthia groped for the latch on her helmet, but Thrutt eased her hand away.

"You need to leave that on," he said. "Rogue pressurized your suit to try to stop the bleeding. Taking the helmet off will break the seal."

"I messed up again," she whispered. Her mouth was dry. "He's going to be mad at me."

Thrutt shook his head. "Don't worry about it. This wasn't you. Someone else must have killed Errol right after we left. I'm sure we aren't the only ones he's toyed with."

"He was lying," Orinthia said.

"Who?"

"The boy." Her throat burned from the recycled oxygen in her suit. "The one who said Errol was dead. He lied."

"So, Errol isn't dead?" Thrutt rubbed his cheek.

Orinthia rolled her head back and forth against the back of her helmet.

"Why would he say that then?"

"To push us on the path he wants us to take."

30

*T*hrutt told Orinthia stories of his home planet, what his house looked like, and shared some of his favorite memories of times with his family. He asked her questions and shook her when she took too long to answer. Staying conscious was a battle he would not let her lose.

Before *Freya* had fully landed, Thrutt scooped Orinthia into his arms and stood at the exit. When the doors opened, he ran with her tucked tightly against his chest so as not to jostle her too much.

Each step he took sent shocks through Orinthia's injury, but she was too weak to care. The movement soothed her, and she fought to stay awake.

"Medic," he shouted as they burst through the med-bay.

The bright lights and white walls stung Orinthia's eyes. She squinted and turned her face toward Thrutt's chest.

"She's been shot," Orinthia heard Thrutt explain. "Her suit is pressurized and I think that's the only thing keeping her from bleeding out."

He gingerly placed her on the table and let her go flat.

Orinthia closed her eyes as the light moved about her

face. It felt nice to keep her eyes shut. She could hear Thrutt and the medic talking, but their voices grew farther away the longer she laid there. Soon, everything was silent, and she let the darkness take her.

HER DREAMS WERE LESS chaotic than they had been. The child versions of her and Kos continued to play in the cemetery, but instead of her father, it was Uri who joined them. He moved in and out of her dream like a spirit, never playing a constant role. Though he tried to speak with the children, Orinthia could not hear his voice. When she moved toward him, he would disappear again.

The green cemetery faded into a bright light. Somewhere in her subconscious, Orinthia wondered if this was how it felt to die. To pass through a dreamlike state, then step into the light. She embraced the stillness and waited to evaporate like her dream, but it did not come.

Slowly, her eyes focused on her surroundings. The memory of where she was trickled in, though not she was not clear on how she got there. Cool, sterile air brushed against her face, helping to draw her senses back to reality. The room was quiet, other than the faint rumble of the engines she decided must have been nearby.

"There you are," someone said. Their voice sent a familiar jolt through her mind. It was an impossible voice, one that was not meant to be where she thought she was.

Orinthia wondered if she really had died and visiting those in her past was part of the process.

"How are you feeling?" The man's voice moved closer.

Orinthia dared not look in hopes the owner would vanish again.

A hand pressed against her forehead. Orinthia drew the courage to move her eyes to meet the golden-brown ones looking down at her.

Uri's eyes had not matched since the accident. It was the one thing Desidario could not replicate perfectly. The difference was not blatantly obvious. But to Orinthia, it was the smallest of details that mattered most.

He smiled at her. The warm smile that filled her with comfort. A smile of pure joy after being apart for long periods of time.

Orinthia squeezed her eyes shut, convinced they deceived her. But when she opened them again, Uri still stood beside her.

"What are you doing here?" she asked hoarsely.

"Saving your life, for starters." Uri lifted her hand and kissed it gently, patting it afterwards.

"I thought I knew where I was, but I'm not so sure now." Using her elbows, she propped herself up and scooted into a seated position. Her abdomen ached and she tightened her muscles around it to keep stiff. Orinthia scanned the room, but her brain refused to believe what her eyes saw.

As if he could read what she was thinking, Uri said, "We're on the *Fera*."

"But how? How did you get here?"

"The usual way." He pulled a stool out from behind her bed and sat down. "Kidnapped."

The word hit her like a slap. "What?"

"I finished my tour of the EC's new lunar facilities for recovering veterans who received cybernetic treatment because of their injuries," Uri said, settling into his seat. "The Navy chartered a flight back for me on one of their ships. A few hours in, we were attacked. The *Fera's* crew must have done some digging through the data, because somehow, they discovered I was a surgeon. One thing led to another, and here I am."

Orinthia tried to wrap her mind around what he said. She was still groggy, and whatever medication Uri gave her had not fully worn off. "When?"

"A little over two weeks ago, I think. I'm not allowed to leave the medical center, so my days are mixed up."

The realization settled in. It was her first raid. He must have been brought on before Xyla was killed. Her stomach turned.

"I had a chat with your friend." Uri looked at her with a raised eyebrow. "He was curious as to how I knew you. After I accused him of kidnapping *you*, he explained everything to me."

The tightness in her stomach grew. "You didn't tell him, did you?"

"That you're a Hunter?"

Orinthia nodded.

"It was part of my accusation." Uri tilted his head and bobbed it up and down. "I thought you and the twins had come to rescue me, and that's how you got hurt."

She closed her eyes and wished to fade away like her dreams. To be dust in the wind and never seen again. "You should have let me die."

"What? Why?" Uri's voice went high.

"Because they are going to kill me. You'll be lucky if they don't kill you, too."

31

*H*ours went by, laughter was shared, and tears were shed. Orinthia retold every moment of her time aboard the *Fera*, sparing no detail. Uri had always been the one person she could completely confide in. The only one who knew all her secrets. He never judged or pitied her. He listened and loved her. And she loved him, though it was never said.

Her tale ended. The room went quiet. Her story was a lot to get through, but she felt better about sharing it with him.

"Do you think Father is a traitor?" she asked, growing uncomfortable with the silence; something she gained from the time spent with Thrutt.

Uri did not answer.

"Was he?" Orinthia's palms started to sweat. The monitor still connected to her beeped a little quicker.

"I don't have concrete evidence he was," Uri explained, holding his hands out with his palms down. "But a lot of things would make more sense if he were a traitor."

"How could we not have known?" Orinthia asked.

+ 135 +

"Maybe we did but couldn't admit it. We were kids. There were things we just didn't understand."

As she was about to agree, footsteps sounded through the med-bay. Ahto and Kos walked in and stopped at the foot of her bed. Kos stood behind the captain with his eyes on the wall, avoiding Orinthia, and arms held behind his back.

"How is our patient, doctor?" Ahto asked. He, too, folded his arms behind him.

"She'll survive," Uri said with ice in his words. He looked at Ahto with disdain.

"Very well," Ahto said. "Then you will release her back to her duties immediately."

Uri opened his mouth, but Orinthia spoke up first. "I'd be glad to get back to work, sir."

"Good." Ahto gave her a quick nod. "Report to Thrutt as soon as you can. He and Rogue have already explained what happened on Rust Rock."

Orinthia froze, not daring to give away any emotion.

"Errol was nothing but a charlatan, and I apologize for the damage his con caused you. It's a shame someone had already killed him before you got there. I would have liked to have done it myself."

The blood drained from Orinthia's face. She did not know what to say. "Yes, sir. Thank you."

Ahto tapped his heels together, gave a bow at the hip, then turned and left.

Kos met Orinthia's eyes for a second, then slid away after his captain.

URI TRIED to convince Orinthia to stay, but she promised she would be back after she found out what was going on. Once she left the med-bay, she hurried for the crew's quarters.

Orinthia tapped her knuckles against the hatch that led to Thrutt's room. It opened to Thrutt standing on the other side. He took a second to register what he saw before scooping her up and hugging her.

A pain shot up her side and caused her to take in a sharp breath.

Thrutt quickly set her down and moved his hands off. "I'm sorry," he repeated until sure she was alright.

"It's okay," Orinthia said. "He told me I'd have some tenderness for a little bit while the nanites repair the damage. It should go away soon."

"Your brother?" Thrutt asked in a whisper.

Orinthia studied his face, but he gave nothing away. "Can I come in?"

Thrutt stepped back as if on a hinge and allowed her to pass. His room was neatly decorated with paintings and sculptures. A photo of four stone creatures hung on the wall above his bed.

Orinthia sat on a chair and looked out his window and waited for him to say something. She knew he was good at breaking the silence.

"Would you have ever told me you were a Hunter?" Thrutt asked.

Without taking her eyes off the stars, she answered, "I don't know. What was I supposed to say? 'Hey, guess what? Remember when you found me drinking my weight in alcohol? Well, I had just lost my job as a Marauder Hunter.' Sounds great."

"I feel like I've been more than transparent enough with you. You could have said *something*."

Orinthia turned herself in the seat and faced him. "The only person I've ever trusted is Uri. Everyone else always wanted to use me in some way. You were a stranger."

"I'm not a stranger now."

She took a deep breath and gave a synopsis of her childhood. That it was true her mother died, and Uri was crushed. How Desidario recreating Uri as a cyborg to save him sparked the drive to reimagine the rest of his children.

Her body shook as she spoke about Adora and Arsenio. She cried as she pieced together the torment they put her through whenever she was forced to expose their lies.

Thrutt held her hands in his cold diamond ones as she relived her teenage years. When she decided she would lie to her father about the twins to save herself from the lashings they dealt. But her own deceit prompted her father to beat the dishonesty out of her. And that led to her hatred for him and realizing she was cursed no matter what she did.

"Why did you stay?" Thrutt asked when Orinthia finished speaking. "Why did you continue to work with them as an adult?"

Orinthia wiped her eyes on her arm. "I had nowhere else to go. My mother would have wanted us to stay together, and I needed to hold on to that small part of her."

Thrutt wagged his head. "Your mother would have wanted you to be happy. She would have never wanted you to suffer, especially not for her sake."

Tired of the ache in her chest, she changed the subject. "What did you and Rogue tell Ahto?"

"It took some convincing, but I got Kos to understand that we needed to keep your secrets as your own until you decide what to do. He had a hard time getting over not telling Ahto you are Desidario's daughter, but I worked it out."

Thrutt continued, "We explained to Ahto that Errol was

nothing but a conman who preyed on desperation and was a master of manipulation. That his ruse must have gotten him killed while we were away. And when the guards found us in there with him, they attacked us."

"But he's not dead," Orinthia said.

"Yes, but we were told he was, and seeing as none of are *supposed* to detect lies, we can leave it at that."

"Does Kos know about Uri?" She could deal with Kos knowing she was Desidario's daughter. But she needed to keep her relation to Uri a secret.

"Only that he is a surgeon contracted by the EC. And I didn't tell him about you being a Hunter, either. Thought it best not to drop too much on him at once."

"Thank you, Thrutt," she said. "You have saved my life more than once."

"You're welcome." Thrutt squeezed her hand tight and gave her a smile.

32

*O*rinthia laid on the bed in her room for hours. She clutched the photo of her mother to her chest and thought of the mistakes she made. Everything she tried to do failed. She was as useless as her sister said. Even being a marauder ended up going poorly.

Her stomach rumbled and begged for food. Uri had done a good job keeping her nourished while she was in the med-bay, but she had eaten nothing solid since on *Freya*. Setting down the framed hologram of her mother, Orinthia gingerly moved her legs over the side of the bed and stood up.

The sound of alarms ringing and warning lights spinning caught her off guard.

"All hands on deck," a voice that did not belong to Kos said. "Report to the observation deck for a vote."

Orinthia wondered if she could get away with skipping the vote because of her condition but decided it would be less of a hassle to just go. She walked to the door and stepped out.

Thrutt was already moving toward her.

"What's going on?" she asked Thrutt when he was closer.

"It's not good," he answered, leading Orinthia to the lift.

"Rogue detected a civilian cruise ship. He was charting a course to avoid it, but Ahto ordered him to track it. When Rogue questioned him, Ahto turned on him and demanded we set to attack it."

"I thought we didn't go after non-military ships," Orinthia said.

"We don't. I left to find you before I could hear the rest."

The walk from the cabins to the observation deck made Orinthia's side burn. She moved with her arm pressed against her middle, hoping to brace the strain. Thrutt walked steadily beside her, ready to help her if needed.

Most of the crew had already assembled on the observation deck before Orinthia and Thrutt arrived. Those that stood closest to the back looked at them as they approached. A few gave sour looks, others sympathetic. Orinthia wondered how much yarn had been spun while she was unconscious.

From the back of the room, she could see Ahto and Kos standing on the platform. Kos's face was twisted and cold, like he was fighting something inside himself. He glanced at the pair and dashed down the steps to them.

"Something is wrong with Ahto," Kos said. "It's like he's glitching. I don't think his programming is meant to last this long."

"What did he say?" Thrutt asked.

"Ahto is frustrated because of what happened on Rust Rock," Kos answered. He looked at Orinthia for a moment, then back to Thrutt. "He's tired of losing. I need both of you to help."

It surprised her when he spoke to her.

"Tell us what you want us to do," Thrutt said.

"Help me convince the others this is wrong," Kos answered. "When the vote is called, vote no. The *people* are not our enemies." He looked at Orinthia again, not with hatred, but with tenderness.

"How are you feeling?" he asked her.

"Better." She patted her side. "Thank you." She meant it both for asking and for saving her.

Kos seemed to understand. He forced a smile, then raced back to the platform.

Ahto called the room to attention as Kos stepped up the stairs. "It has been too long since your service has gone unpaid. We have suffered too many failures as of late. How would you like an opportunity to get what you deserve?"

The crowd shouted in affirmation.

"Remember who it was that cast you away," Ahto shouted. "It wasn't just the Confederacy. It was the people. Who remembers coming home and being shunned by those we swore to protect? The disgusted faces when they noticed our marks of war? Families who were conditioned to believe the tech we possessed, the tech thrust upon us, was dirty and evil. How many of you were asked to remove a mod to make others feel safe?"

The crew was hot. They shifted around, squirming at the memories Ahto dragged up.

"They demanded you change who you were to fit into society again, when you had done nothing wrong," Ahto continued. "It was them that pushed the EC policies and enforced their gross 'anti-war tech' rhetoric. It is them that should pay as well."

A hush fell over the room. Ahto was losing them at the mention of attacking civilians. Some of the crew still bounced, ready to fight, but others whispered to each other.

"There is a ship transporting financiers of the war," Ahto spoke with crescendo. "Now is our chance to show them what their money paid for. Reveal ourselves to those who cast us aside and turned their backs, those who protested at our return home. Make them know that we will not fade quietly into history. We will show them we should be honored and feared. They should celebrate us for our sacrifices and hold us high, for we were low. Stand up and take back what is yours. Make them see you."

Cheers and shouts broke out. Ahto won them over. Some pounded their chests; others stomped their feet. It was electric. The room would burst with energy soon, and there would be no way to contain the blast.

"This is not our way of doing things," Kos shouted over the voices. He climbed on top of the banister. "We have never attacked civilians before. They are not the real enemy. The EC made them believe lies about us. If we do this, those lies will be reinforced. We will never be able to come back from it. These are those we vowed to protect."

"We honored those vows," Ahto shouted. He shifted to his snake form and came to Kos' height. "They no longer bind us."

Orinthia could hardly hear the two argue over the noise. She tried to pass her own objections, but the cheers drowned out her voice as well.

Ahto turned to face the crowd. His voice boomed over the rest. "Now we vote. All for?"

Hands flew up around the room.

"Against?"

Only three voted. Kos. Orinthia. Thrutt.

"Gunners, prepare your boarding parties," Ahto said with a venomous grin. "Today we enter a new chapter in our lives. Today, we will make them listen to us."

Orinthia and Thrutt were caught in the torrent of marauders rushing over the observation deck. Thrutt took hold of her and held her behind him, shielding her so she would not get trampled.

Someone grabbed her hand and pulled her from Thrutt's grip. Her skin burned at the touch, but she did not resist. Kos dragged her out of the way into a connecting corridor. Thrutt followed behind and used his back to block others from running their direction.

"We can't let them do this," Kos said when they were all together. "I will not be part of slaughtering innocents again."

"Can we try to warn the other ship?" Orinthia asked. "If we can get to the comms room and hail them, maybe they'll turn around before they get too close."

"It could work," Thrutt said. "Worth a shot."

"Fine," Kos said. "Thrutt, you go with the others and monitor everything. Stall or do whatever it takes to keep them from going through with this. Thia and I will go to the comms room."

Thrutt looked out into the corridor. "It's clear. Good luck." He stepped away and ran after their crew mates. His heavy feet pounded the steel as he did.

"Are you sure you want to do this?" Orinthia asked. "I don't think Ahto will forgive this level of insubordination."

Kos looked at her for a moment. He did not have the fire or the smoldering embers in his eyes. They were still full of pain, but something had changed. "I've done things out of duty that will haunt me until the day I die. It's time I do things because it is the right thing to do, not because someone orders me to."

$\mathcal{K}$os moved through the ship with ease. It was his home for as long as it had existed. As far as Orinthia knew, he could have had a hand in the design. He moved in the shadows, avoiding the rest of the crew until he and Orinthia stopped outside the comms room.

The doors flew open as Kos moved forward. Orinthia kept close to his heels in case the doors closed on her, unsure if she had access to the room or not.

The four marauders sitting inside at their consoles looked at their quartermaster with confusion.

"Establish communications with the civilian ship," Kos said. He spoke with a force that could shake a mountain.

They exchanged looks, but no one moved to follow his command.

"That is an order," Kos barked.

One operator slowly flicked a few switches and typed in something on a panel. "Link established," he said.

"Hello? Who is this?" a grumpy, old voice asked. The face it belonged to appeared on the screen in the center of the room. He was pudgy in the neck, but the skin sagged around his cheeks. The man squinted through a pair of half rimmed glasses.

"This is the *Fera*," Kos announced. "We will attack your ship within the hour if you do not turn around now."

The man chuckled. "The *Fera*? Who is that?"

Kos sucked in air like someone had punched him in the gut. "We are a crew of one hundred-fifty marauders. All who are ready to disable and board your ship."

"Marauders? No, I don't think so. The GMH guaranteed us safe passage. There are no marauders in this sector. Besides, there is nothing on our radar. Please disconnect the line. I have a schedule to keep."

The screen went blank. Everyone in the room stared at Kos. He had just committed mutiny, and they all witnessed it.

Orinthia stepped closer to him and spoke so only he could hear. "What now?"

Kos closed his eyes.

Orinthia saw his eyelids twitch as if she could see his brain working.

"Come on," Kos said as he ran from the communication room.

He and Orinthia raced down more halls toward the shipping bay. "Where are we going?" Orinthia asked. "We can't fly out there in time. Ahto will see us leave."

"He will," Kos said, passing the entrance to the hold. "But we can disable the cannons long enough for the other ship to get out of range."

Orinthia remembered the ion cannons they used on the EC ship. "How?"

Kos stopped a few paces before another door so not to trigger the auto-open. "The cannons are on self-maintenance. But we could overload the controls so it takes a while for it to function again."

"You don't look so sure," Orinthia said. "Why?"

"The Master Gunner, Neve," he answered. His voice was hollow.

The door to the weapons room slid open. Orinthia turned around to see a tall woman step out, as if summoned. She was almost as tall as Thrutt and wore a purple coat that brushed the ground as she walked out of the room. Her thin black hair trailed down to her waist, accenting her sickly grey flesh that clung to her bones.

"Maurice from the comms room warned you might come here next," Neve said. Her voice was raspy and hurt Orinthia's ears. "You're not going near those cannons." With a stomp of her foot, two long swords jumped out of her leg. The blades hung in the air for a moment before she swung her arms around, grabbed hold of the hilts, and stood her ground.

Orinthia crossed her arms and thrust out her own blades. Her side ached from the movement. She panted from the run, but she did not flinch.

"I don't want to fight you, Neve." Kos held out his hand in front of him with the palms down. "Ahto is malfunctioning and making crazy decisions."

"You've always been too lofty," Neve said. She wagged her onyx-colored hair. "So *honorable*, like you're better than the rest of us. But we both know what you're capable of. What you've done."

Kos stiffened his jaw but did not answer back.

"How many lives have you snuffed out? How many haunt you when you sleep? This is who we are, Rogue."

"I was only following orders," Kos said. "It was my job. We are free of those orders now."

"Nothing has changed," Neve spat out. "We have only gone from government sanctioned killing to freelancers." She slid her feet apart and held the points of her swords out.

Kos tossed off his coat and ran a hand over his arm. Before Orinthia could focus on what happened, copper colored armor plating resembling his tattoo formed over his body. It assembled in sequence up from his hands to his neck. The shield he used to scan her injuries earlier slammed down over his eyes and connected with the plating over his head.

The sudden transformation distracted Orinthia enough to miss Neve's lunge at her.

Kos threw his arm out between her sword and Orinthia's head. The sound of metal on metal made Orinthia's ears ring. Drawn into the moment, she drew her leg up and sent a kick into Neve's knee.

The woman stumbled back but regained her balance. Neve growled from her chest like a wild animal and dashed forward.

This time, Orinthia was ready and caught the movement with her own blades. They swung at each other, dodging blows. Every strike hurt the wound in her side, making it hard to concentrate.

Orinthia stopped to catch her breath. Neve, however, was not impaired and took the opportunity to slash at her.

Again, Kos used his body to deflect it. Sparks flew as Neve ran a sword across his chest. As the blade made its final pass, he gripped the hilt and yanked it away.

"Take care of the cannons," he shouted to Orinthia. "We are running out of time."

Orinthia jumped out from behind him. She blocked Neve's sword as she ran past and made it to the door of the weapons room. It did not open. She looked back at Kos but did not want to shout her problem.

Kos glanced at her and gave a swift nod. He feverishly swung at Neve and drove her back a few steps. When she was close enough, the doors opened.

Orinthia ran through and looked around. Lights and switches flashed at her. She had no idea how to use what she saw. With a reverse cross, she retracted one of her blades and pressed everything she could touch. Nothing happened. *Locked*, she thought.

The image of the civilian ship blinked on the radar. They were just outside the green circle in the middle of the screen. Numbers above the screen counted down their approach.

Orinthia rushed back for the exit, slammed on the release switch, and stepped into the corridor.

Kos lay on the ground. The sword he took from Neve was at his feet. Neve stood over him with the point of her sword aimed right at his center.

Without thinking, Orinthia ran forward with the blade she kept out, and lunged at Neve. The martian steel slid through her like a hot knife through butter. Before Orinthia could pull her arm back, Neve toppled sideways, snapping Orinthia's blade at the seam.

Kos scurried away from his fallen crew mate and stared at the two women. With a reverse swipe on his arm, the armor retreated, and he was normal.

34

"*T*he controls are jammed," Orinthia said. Her voice was detached and sounded far away to her ears. She could not take her eyes off the dead woman with Orinthia's broken blade protruding out from her back.

Kos cleared the distance to her and placed his fiery hands on either side of her face, forcing her to look away. "Don't let it in."

"I she—." Her words broke off.

"No. No. You saved me. There is a difference." Kos pulled her head up so he could look her in the eye. "We need to save the ship. Stay with me."

Orinthia's body rattled to the core as she attempted to nod.

Kos let go of her face and turned toward the cannon room. "Show me what you did."

Her voice was hollow as she explained how she pushed everything she could reach. Then, she pointed to the screen and showed him how close the other ship was.

"Neve must have already locked them," Kos said. "They'll automatically fire when the ship is in range."

"So that's it?" Orinthia asked, emotion building in her eyes. "Aren't you Quartermaster? Can't you override it or something?" *This has to work*, she thought. *I did not do all of this for nothing.*

Kos pressed his head against the wall and closed his eyes. "Only Ahto can make changes during a battle. The system will only work for him and Neve."

"What are we going to do?" Orinthia's voice wavered.

"The cannons can be adjusted manually," he answered low.

"How?" Orinthia looked around, hoping to see the words "Manual Controls" written somewhere she might have missed.

"From outside." Kos lifted his head and turned so his bottom rested on the console. "There are two cannons on the starboard side. We'll both have to move them."

The floor seemed to fall out underneath Orinthia. She heard what he said but wished she hadn't. Swallowing hard, she said, "I need my suit. I think it is still in the med-bay." The thought of going back to Uri after what she had done scared her more than having to step outside of a moving ship to direct a cannon by hand.

"We'll go together," Kos said. "My armor can double as an emergency self-contained suit. I don't want to get separated."

Her heart pounded with every step as they ran toward Uri. Orinthia wanted to throw up.

She and Kos skidded into the medical center and searched for the spacesuit and mag boots. They tossed the room apart and looked under every bed.

Uri stepped out of his back quarters, holding a steaming mug. "Wh—." He paused. "What happened to your arm?"

Orinthia's eyes followed his gaze down. She had

forgotten to change it back to her normal arm after the blade broke off.

"Where is my suit?" she asked, swinging her arm to fix it. "The one I was brought in with a few days ago."

"Why? What's going on?" Uri moved his focus between his sister and Kos.

Orinthia tried her best to explain the situation, skipping the part where she fought and killed Neve.

"That's too dangerous," Uri shouted and moved his hands. A splash of tea dripped to the floor. "You can't go out there. Even if you hadn't just been shot. I won't let you."

Kos spoke up, "We appreciate you doing your job and honoring your oath. But it isn't up to you what she does."

Uri slammed his cup down on a table and glared at Kos. "I've been invested in her wellbeing for a while."

Orinthia shot him a warning look and said through tight lips, "Give me my suit. People are going to die if we don't try."

Her brother left the room with a sigh. A moment later, he returned holding her spacesuit and boots. "As a medical professional, I have to warn you against this. There is still blood inside here."

Orinthia snatched her things out of his hands and tried not to think about it as she stepped into the suit. The dried blood flaked and dusted off where it rubbed against her, but it was not as bad as she thought it would have been.

"Be careful, please," Uri shouted as Orinthia and Kos ran out of the med-center.

Orinthia sealed her helmet and was ready to go by the time they reached the repair hatch.

Kos punched in a code, and the porthole slid aside. The airlock kept them from getting sucked out into the void.

"Turn on your boots before going out," Kos said. "The ship is still moving, so you'll drift away if you don't."

Orinthia bent down to turn on the mags. A yellow light flashed on the button. "The charge is low."

Kos cursed. "We'll have to do this quickly, then. When you get outside, go left and head straight for the cannon. I'll instruct you from there." He swiped at his armor tattoo and once again was engulfed in his armor. "Can you hear me?" His voice was muffled.

"Yes."

"Okay, go."

With a hand clasped to the edge of the opening, Orinthia pulled herself out. Still holding onto the side, she brought a foot up and attached it to the hull. It was a strange sensation, being sideways without gravity. Her mind could not make sense of it. Planting the other foot, she moved steadily to her target.

"I'm here," she said, taking hold of the cannon a few minutes later.

"There should be an orange lever on the side of the cannon," Kos told her. "Like the one Thrutt used to detach the winch. Stand behind the cannon and pull the handle toward you. That will disengage the lock."

Orinthia strained herself as she pulled. She wished she had asked Uri to give her something for the pain before leaving him. The lever shifted back and gave way. "Done." She panted.

"Come back around and push it up as far as you can. That will put it in its docking position. Don't let go until you hear it click." Kos struggled as he spoke.

With every bit of effort she had, Orinthia pushed against the weapon. Her injury sent white light to her vision, and she feared the hole would pop open at any moment. "It's stuck." She did not hear Kos' response.

An alarm blared inside her ears. Orinthia looked down at her boots, which flashed red. Her feet slipped from the ship and lifted off. She gripped the cannon, but her gloved hands slid against the smooth surface.

The two cannons were too far apart, and she knew Kos would not reach her in time.

"Rogue, I want to tell you your sacrifice was worth it," Orinthia said, trying to mask the terror in her voice. "You won a war no one expected you to win, and you came home to thankless masses. You are a real hero. I'm sorry for what I said back on *Freya*. Please tell Thrutt and Uri I'm sorry, too."

He did not answer. Maybe it was for the best.

The last bit of cannon slipped from under her hand, and Orinthia floated away from the *Fera*. She closed her eyes and pictured herself sitting on the grass beside her mother's grave, cool air from beneath the trees blowing through her hair. *There will be no grave for me*, she thought.

Uri would know. Somehow, that did not give her much comfort. Orinthia wondered what would happen to him. Would Thrutt make sure he was taken care of?

As the peace and stillness of the expanse settled on her, she felt a hand tug at her foot, dragging her back to the hull. With a smile, Orinthia looked down, expecting to see Kos at her rescue. The feeling of relief quickly turned to terror when she saw it was not Kos who had her.

It was Ahto.

35

*T*here was no strength left to fight against the arms that held Orinthia tightly. Her body ached, and she was adrenaline fatigued. The marauders dragged her part of the way since she could hardly stand as they made their way to the brig.

Kos, however, thrashed like a caught beast. It took three crew members to keep him from breaking loose. One for each arm and one for both his legs. They held him suspended in the air, forced into a swan dive.

Ahto walked up front. He strode with his hands behind his back and head held high. They were the only group that walked this part of the ship.

Orinthia assumed the rest were preparing to attack the civilian cruise liner. Her heart sank again. They tried so hard yet failed even harder. Everything she did was for nothing, and if she had not been so tired, she would have cried.

The prisoners were tossed into a cell. Orinthia laid on her side and pulled her legs close to her chest.

Kos kicked off the ground and rushed for the barred door.

Ahto slammed it right as Kos crossed the threshold. The force of it sent him backward, leaving a red mark down his face.

"Did you think no one would tell me?" Ahto sneered as he spoke. "Neve is dead. I would not have thought you had it in you after the show you put on before."

Orinthia refused to acknowledge he spoke to her. She stared at his boots and took in long drags of air through her nose.

"Whose idea was it to betray me?" Ahto asked.

"Mine," Kos said. A bruise already formed where he hit the pole and blood streamed out of his nose. He slid himself up and put his back against the wall. The prison was barely wide enough for his legs to stretch all the way out. "I'm tired of following leaders who think lives don't hold equal weight on a scale. Who are we to decide who lives or dies?"

Ahto crouched down and peered through the spaces in the door. "I decide. That is why I was created. To calculate the cost of life. And you were *recreated* to kill. That is your purpose."

Orinthia caught Kos glance at her, then back to Ahto. "We can choose our own path. I may have been given these mods to kill, but I can refuse to use them to serve the will of others. My family owed a debt to the Navy. That is why I joined. Killing was not my goal. It was to save lives."

"And look what they did to you." Ahto stood up again and looked down his nose at Kos.

Kos lifted his own head. "I can't help what they did to me. But I can decide what I do about it. And I will no longer give my peace for someone else's war."

Ahto and the other five marauders laughed. "You may not have much time left, anyway. After we take the transport ship, we will vote on what to do with the two of you. Wish us luck." The marauders parted for Ahto to walk through, then turned on their heels and left with him.

Orinthia forced herself to sit upright and scooted closer to Kos so she, too, could stretch out her legs. She looked up and could see through a porthole in the ceiling. Her eyes closed and she rested in silence. Kos breathed loudly beside her. She could feel the heat come off his body. "What's going to happen?" Orinthia asked.

Kos shifted beside her. His voice sounded like he was looking up, too, but she did not open her eyes to be sure. "After they take the ship, Ahto will probably have us marooned."

"Marooned?" Orinthia choked. She dropped her head and looked at him. "Like leave us on a deserted planet?"

He nodded. "He has a favorite picked out. We sent a few of our former captains to meet their maker there in the early days." Kos let his head fall to the side and looked her in the eye. "With the life I've lived, I can't say I'm surprised I go out this way."

"I thought we got left on inhabited planets?" Orinthia asked.

"This is mutiny," Kos answered. "Mutiny is different. It is personal to Ahto."

Orinthia moved her lips over her teeth. "What about Thrutt? What will happen to him? Won't Ahto assume he was in on it, too?"

"He'd be in here already if Ahto had. If Thrutt is smart, he'll vote against us to save face."

Orinthia could not believe what he told her. Her time on the *Fera* had been a whirlwind to say the least. They stared at each other. She could see something working behind his eyes, but she did not know what.

"Thank you," Kos said with a soft voice. "And I'm sorry, too."

His statement confused her. Had he heard her apologies? "For what?"

"Thank you for showing me it doesn't matter what the Navy made me to be; I have the freedom to use my mods my way." Kos paused and chewed the inside of his lip. "And I'm sorry for treating you so harshly. To stand against authority when they are wrong is not a weakness. It threatened my point of view, and I lashed out."

Orinthia could see Thrutt in him as he spoke. The kindness and transparency he tried to instill in both of them. "I have something I have to tell you."

Kos made a half smile. "There'll be plenty of time for deathbed confessions. Save it for then."

Orinthia sighed and looked up through the porthole at the expanse. There was no point in telling him about her former job anymore, other than to make her feel better. It would not change their circumstances.

A bright light flashed across the window. The entire ship shook and alarms rang out. Orinthia bumped into Kos.

"What was that?" she asked, straightening herself.

"Something hit us." Kos stood up and looked out the view.

"Did the transporter have weapons?" Orinthia lifted herself onto her feet with one hand on the wall and the other on her side.

"I don't think so."

The ship rocked again. Kos caught Orinthia before she fell forward. They were definitely under attack.

Orinthia moved her head around, trying to get a better angle. But it was unnecessary. A prestigious white ship with large blue fins and the words MHS *Mathias* came into view. She gasped. "Hunters."

"How did they find us?" Kos craned his neck.

Her mind raced. The *Mathias* was not just a Hunter ship; it was their flagship. The one the twins commanded.

36

A barrage of cannon fire hit the *Fera*, rattling Orinthia in her bones. She had sat down again and leaned forward to keep her head from beating against the wall. The sound of the *Mathias'* constant attack made her momentarily deaf. She had not realized Kos spoke to her until he jabbed her in the arm.

"Don't worry," he shouted. "The shields will hold. They'll have to come aboard to do any actual damage."

That was exactly what Orinthia feared. It all overwhelmed her. Her two near death incidents. Imprisonment. The attack. The twins found her even after she ran so far away.

Things went quiet again, and they ceased rocking. She could think clearly.

Uri could be rescued, she thought. It was the only silver lining.

"How do you think they found us?" Kos asked.

Orinthia looked up as if she had forgotten he was there. His question slowly registered in her mind. "Maybe one of the crew on the other ship had some sense and radioed for backup just in case. Their captain said Hunters promised safe passage. They were probably nearby. The GMH has been looking for the *Fera* for a while."

Kos ran his tongue against the inside of his cheek. "Do you think we can pull off being real captives? Locked away in here, they wouldn't know the difference, right?"

The thought had crossed her mind before he spoke it. Would Adora or Arsenio believe they had kidnapped her? The likelihood of convincing them of anything was not high. Even if she really had been a captive, they would probably throw her in prison on marauding charges just so they would not have to deal with her anymore.

"We best not push our luck," Orinthia said, realizing his question had gone unanswered for a over a minute.

"Yeah, figured it would be worth the shot."

Orinthia's mind drifted to her first day aboard the *Fera* and how she got lost in the maze of corridors. Depending on where they boarded, it could take them forever to get to Uri.

Again, the ship shook, but differently than before. This time, it was from a return fire on the port side.

"They probably haven't gotten the starboard cannons back online, yet," Kos said, sitting beside her with one knee up and his arm draped over it. "I wish I could see what was happening. This is agonizing."

"Thrutt told me about your childhood." Orinthia lifted her knees and laid her head against them so she could look at him. The spacesuit she still wore was cool against her cheek. She let her eyes run over the tattoos on his bare arms.

Kos fiddled with a compass tattoo on his palm and chuckled. "And he told me about yours."

They gently laughed for a few seconds, the sound of which was awkward in the hollow prison.

"Does he know how to keep secrets?" Orinthia asked.

"Hardly." Kos sighed. "I'm glad he found someone else to talk to besides me, though. He loves the company."

"He is so kind," Orinthia said. "Not the quality one looks for in a marauder. Why is he here?"

Kos pinched his lips together and twisted his face. "Me. My aunt died two years after Thrutt and I joined the Navy. We are all each other has left. And when he makes a promise, he keeps it."

"And why are you here?" Orinthia found it odd to speak to Kos so much after the rocky start they had.

"I had nowhere else to go," he answered.

Her mod hummed. "You're lying."

Kos looked away from her and down at his hands. He traced the outline of the compass with his finger. "War is ugly. You would think that soldiers would be the major casualties, but they aren't. It's civilians. The enemy will hold up in a settlement or commandeer a passenger ship. And instead of doing precision warfare, it's generally decided that destroying the opposition at all costs outweighs the 'few' innocent lives lost."

He took a breath and licked his lips before speaking again. "My father abandoned his post and left a debt to the Navy. I agreed to pay the debt so my aunt could finally live in peace. I paid off his balance and added four years of my own. When you enlist, you are theirs to wield. Neve was right. There are ghosts that haunt me from the lives I took in the name of peace. So, when Ahto asked me to join his crew, I felt like I had no other choice but to keep doing what I was remade to do."

Orinthia let the silence hang between them. She understood how much effort it took to face the truth and gave him the space to recover.

It was short-lived, however. For though the volley had continued to sway and rattle the ship, a louder, heftier explosion sounded.

Red and white lights flashed. A high-pitched screech sounded through the speakers.

"The Hunters have breached." Kos lifted his head. "The ship will auto-patch the airlock, but they'll be able to come aboard."

In her mind's eye, Orinthia pictured Adora dressed in her black and teal uniform leading her team through a hole in the hull. Arsenio would follow with a second wave, and they would comb through the ship, taking prisoners and killing anyone who opposed them.

Her pulse quickened. She did not want to see them. She did not want to explain what she was doing on a marauder vessel. There had to be some way out.

Orinthia jumped up and frantically pulled at the bars. "We have to get out." Even she could hear the panic in her voice. "Shoot the lock. Do something."

"Ahto would have already deactivated my access to everything. It really isn't that hard."

Orinthia spun around and looked at him. "You said Thrutt told you about my past. Well, that past is about to find me. The only thing they hate more than me is marauders."

Kos tilted his head to the side and squinted. "The twins that tortured you as a kid are Hunters?"

"Obviously, that's what I'm saying," she said, fanning her fingers out for effect. "And so was I up until a few weeks ago. Use your imagination to think about how they'll react when they see me here, because your guess is as good as mine."

Kos pressed his fingers to his forehead and closed his

eyes. "Of course. You know, a lot of things make more sense, now."

Orinthia grunted and kicked the wall. "I can explain everything some other time. But right now, I'm terrified."

37

There should have been a groove carved through the floor where Orinthia paced. She moved back and forth like a caged animal, glancing at the brig's entrance every few steps. Her feet were numb from walking the length of the cell for fifteen minutes.

No one had come in. Not Ahto. Not Thrutt. Not Adora or Arsenio. It was almost as if Kos and Orinthia did not exist.

"Can you just try to shoot it?" Orinthia groaned.

"I've already told you five times. No." Kos stood with his back on the wall, staring at his boots. "The air is negatively charged so blasters don't fire in here."

Orinthia let out a scream and kicked the bars. She was thankful the dead mag boots were still on her feet. "This is your ship," she grumbled. "You have to know something about it that can help."

"If I did, I would have already done it." Kos sighed. "We designed the brig so no one could escape. Why would we want a faulty prison?"

"So *we* can get out!" Orinthia stopped pacing and pointed at her chest then Kos'.

"Being locked in my own cell was not something I planned on. And even if we could get out of the cell, our access would have been suspended by now. The doors won't open for us."

Orinthia's legs wobbled. Her stomach and head ached. She still had not eaten.

Just as hopelessness crept up on her, a loud crash caught her off guard. Orinthia stepped back and looked at the main hatch to the room. Thrutt rushed in through the doors that still opened for him.

"I came around the corner too fast and clipped the wall," he explained, though no one had asked.

Kos and Orinthia watched him in surprise.

"What?" he asked, looking down and patting himself. "Is there something on me?"

"I didn't think you'd come," Orinthia stated.

Thrutt's mouth popped open. "Give me a break, you two. There were a lot of places to look through. And if you haven't noticed, a battle is going on out there." He pointed his thumb behind him.

The prisoners exchanged side glances, then looked back at Thrutt.

"Get back," he said. Taking a running start, the stone creature's diamond hands formed into fists in front of him and he charged at the cell door. The impact rattled the floor and left the bar bent. He repeated the movement three more times until the bar snapped from the pressure. Thrutt grabbed hold of the broken pieces and forced one up and the other down, creating enough space for Kos and Orinthia to get through.

Orinthia looked at Thrutt's hands as she went past him. There was a chip missing in one of his knuckles. She placed her hands around his. "I'm sorry I doubted you."

He took his free hand and sandwiched hers. "I came for Rogue, but I guess you can join us." He winked at her.

She realized that not only had Thrutt influenced Kos, but Kos impacted him just as much. They took their broken families and pieced together a new one that may never be perfect, but it was theirs.

Orinthia blinked a tear out of her eye before more could follow it. "Can you take me to the med-bay?"

Kos turned around. "What? We need to get to *Freya* so we can escape."

Thrutt ignored Kos and nodded. "Stay close. The Hunters have rounded up a few of us already."

Again, the door opened for Thrutt. Kos and Orinthia darted through before it could shut on them. They followed him down hallways, sticking to quieter paths.

Sounds of skirmishes echoed around them. Blaster fire and swords connecting rang like bells in all directions. There were screams, too, but Orinthia tried not to imagine who they belonged to. She knew those on both sides of the battle and did not want their faces in her head.

Kos, Orinthia, and Thrutt made it unseen to the medical center. Thrutt entered first, clearing the way.

"Uri!" Orinthia shouted as soon as she was through the doors.

There was no answer. She shouted again.

Before she could call out a third time, Uri stuck his head out from his backroom. "What is going on out there?" he asked.

"It's a long story, but we have to get you out." Orinthia rushed to him and pulled him to where the others stood. "Adora and Arsenio are here. They can take you back home."

"You have to come, too," Uri said, clutching her arm. "This isn't a safe lifestyle."

Orinthia shook her head. "I can't give them the power to use or hurt me anymore, but you belong back on Earth. You help people."

"I'm going with you, then," Uri said. "You're impulsive and make poor decisions. Look where you are!"

Orinthia wanted to laugh. She wanted to say yes, he could come. To fit her broken family in with Kos and Thrutt, traveling the stars free from everything. Yet she knew he would not fit in with her new life. He was still too much a part of the black-and-white world. Her band of outcast marauders needed to blend into the grey areas.

Her mouth opened, but she could say nothing. On the other side of the crystal-clear glass that separated the med-bay from the rest of the ship was the face of her tormentor.

Adora stared at the people inside. Her teeth were clenched so tightly, they looked like they could break from the force at any moment. She raised her rifle and fired two times into the panel that controlled the auto sensors.

Sparks flew into the room. Uri covered Orinthia's head and pressed her against his chest. Thrutt jumped in front of them and spread out his arms to block them from being hit. Kos swiped up his armor and pressed his hips to call his golden blasters.

Orinthia poked her head out from under Uri's arm and looked around Thrutt.

The doors snapped open for Adoracion Anton, and she stepped through. The red scar under her eye stood out like a badge. It was the one thing Orinthia had been able to repay her sister with; though if asked, she would swear it was an accident.

Adora gripped her gun with both hands, but stood with her feet apart, like she was in command of the room. "You're all under arrest," she ordered. "Stand down, or you will be forced to comply."

Kos shouted curses at her, but she did not bat an eye. She raised her palm parallel with Kos. A needle-like dart shot out of her hand and hit him square in the chest. He made a noise, then toppled forward.

38

*T*he ringing of Kos's suit smacking the steel floor had not stopped by the time Adoracion lifted her rifle and aimed at Thrutt's chest. She did not squint or glare at him. Her face was as stony as his.

Orinthia forced her way out of Uri's hold and flung out her good blade. She screamed, which left her throat sore, and dashed to Adora.

Thrutt lunged forward to grab her, but Orinthia dodged his hands.

With her blade pulled back, Orinthia swung forward and slashed across the air at her sister.

Adora jumped back and used her rifle to deflect the attack. She let Orinthia lean into her, then pushed her back, causing her to stumble.

Orinthia regained her footing and swiped again. She continued to swing as she stepped forward, the silver of her blade catching the light as she did.

Though Adora successfully blocked the blows, she held her gun defensively and could not move it into a firing position. Bits of metal flew off her rifle blaster with every strike.

The frantic swinging lasted only minutes. Orinthia stumbled back to catch her breath. The wound in her side burned. Her sister, who had barely exerted any energy during the onslaught, whipped the rifle around and clipped Orinthia in the chin.

A bright light flashed in front of Orinthia's eyes. Her teeth snapped shut, sending a shooting pain through her jaw. This sent her back enough for Thrutt to reach out and grab her while still defending Uri, who was tending to Kos on the ground. He ripped her backward and tossed her behind him.

Orinthia's blade scraped along the floor as she slid on her back across the deck. She lay on the cool surface and tried to gain her bearings.

Adora did not advance or shoot. She stood her ground, eyeing those in front of her. "What a sorry lot this is."

Orinthia rolled to her side and made a rude gesture to her sister.

"Child," Adora spit out the word like it was poison. "Why am I not surprised to find you here?"

Words failed to come forward. Orinthia tried to find the strength to get back up. Her body was tired and worn. She could only stare at the sideways version of Adoracion.

"Whatever." Adora let out a sharp sigh. "This is your last warning. Stand down or I will force you to do so."

"I need to help him, Adora," Uri said. "You hurt him."

"He'll be fine," she snapped. "It is only a paralysis serum. Step away from him and get over here."

Uri looked at Orinthia, then back to Adoracion. "She didn't do anything. They kidnapped her when they kidnapped me. Don't arrest her."

Orinthia's head hummed.

"I don't need her gift to tell me you're lying," Adora said. "When we found her apartment empty, I figured she was either dead in a dump somewhere or had joined the scum. I didn't think it would be this scum, though."

"She told me what you put her through," Thrutt said, drawing attention to himself. "You're a horrible person."

Adora cocked her head to the side. "So, she's started crying to strangers instead of drinking herself to sleep, huh? That's a change. Not sure which is more pathetic."

"What your father did to all of you had nothing to do with her," Thrutt said. "She was a child and had no control."

"We were all children," Adora shouted. Her scar blazed red. Bits of hair poked out of her bun. "The rest of us grew up and accepted our gifts. She didn't."

"Do you blame her? You tortured her. How could she accept herself when you made her believe she was worthless?"

"I don't have to stand here and listen to a talking boulder," Adora said. "Uri, get up or I'll arrest you, too."

Uri slapped the ground in defeat and stood up from beside Kos.

Orinthia lifted herself with her normal hand and stood up. With legs that rattled, she moved to Thrutt's side and watched Uri step closer to their sister.

Without warning, Uri crouched down and lunged at Adora's weapon. She yelled. A light flashed from her blaster. Uri flew backward and landed a foot from where Kos was.

The room froze.

There was no sound other than the pounding in Orinthia's chest. She was not sure she believed what her eyes saw.

Uri lay sprawled out motionless on the ground. Wires stuck out through the hole in his chest. His shirt had burned edges around the wound. Blue liquid seeped from the tubes and puddled around him.

"You killed him!" Orinthia screamed until her throat felt

like it would bleed. Her legs gave out and she dropped to the ground and reached for him. Her hands felt detached from her body as she touched his shoulder. The room was light and full of air, but somehow Orinthia's lungs could not get enough.

Adora did not look away from Uri. Her eyes were wide and mouth ajar. The blaster in her hand was still pointed at the spot Uri stood seconds before.

The scent of burned fabric and synthetic flesh lingered in the air. It smelled of plastic and fibers melting together.

A set of footsteps rushed into the medical center. Orinthia looked up to see Arsenio stand behind his twin. His face was pale, like all the blood had drained from it. He looked at Uri, then let his eyes drift to his youngest sister.

None of them said anything. Orinthia knew Adora must have been silently telling him what happened, if she hadn't already. Arsenio put a hand on Adora's shoulder and guided her back into the corridor. With a final look back at the mess, they turned away and ran from the room.

Orinthia stayed glued to the floor. She brushed the hair from Uri's face and stroked the top of his head. His eyes were closed, and if she had only seen his face, she would have assumed he was sleeping.

The gears in his chest kept spinning. Orinthia wanted to reach in and stop them so he could rest in peace, but she could not bring herself to do it.

Minutes passed. Thrutt bent down beside her. "I'm so sorry, but we have to leave. There is still Ahto to worry about."

Orinthia shook her head. "I can't abandon him while he's dying." Tears pricked at her cheeks. He had saved her when she was at her lowest, but she could not save him.

"There is nothing we can do. He wanted you to be safe."

"He's not dead," Kos said from behind them. His voice was muffled.

The room had been so chaotic, Orinthia forgot he was there. She looked back to see him with his shield still over his face.

"Cyborgs have a different nervous system," Kos continued. He did not move, but the effects of the serum must have worn off enough to allow him to talk. "The head is what controls the body. They don't have hearts like we do. If his head is okay, which I can see it is, then he is just damaged. Not dead."

39

They waited long enough for Kos to regain control of his legs before leaving the med-bay. He deactivated his armor, and Orinthia allowed him to lean on her. His body heat scorched her side, but she ignored it. Thrutt carried Uri.

Orinthia's mind and movements were slow. She had given everything she could. The still-healing wound she arrived with throbbed her waist. Every step was dreadful, but she pressed on until they reached the end of the hall.

Thrutt let Kos and Orinthia stop for a rest while he went forward a little more.

Kos stepped back and put his weight on a railing behind him, giving Orinthia a moment.

The corridor was quiet. Orinthia's arms were exhausted and almost too weak to move. If she blinked too long, she was afraid she would fall asleep where she stood. Her body shook with tiny tremors and felt heavy under her skin.

Thrutt came back and nodded his head for them to follow.

Orinthia placed an arm around Kos's middle again. He

moved more steadily as they made the last walk to where *Freya* waited.

Red and white lights strobed inside the docking bay. It hurt Orinthia's eyes. Through a squint, she could see the shadow of a man standing between them and their destination. Her feet faltered, causing Kos to stumble.

As the beacon passed from red to white, the shadow morphed into a tall, thin snake. His metallic skin reflected the beams, scattering light around him.

Orinthia trembled. There was no fight left in her. If he wanted to attack them, she would have no choice but to surrender.

"I had no idea there were so many turncoats on my ship," Ahto said, slithering toward them until he was a few feet away. "Was *this* part of your plan?"

Kos let his arm drop from Orinthia's shoulder and staggered forward. "We didn't call the Hunters, if that's what you're getting at. I wanted to stop you from taking innocent lives, not betray you."

Ahto hissed. His eyes caught a glint of the red light. "Half my crew has been arrested. Another dozen killed. Now I find my quartermaster escaping. It looks like betrayal to me."

"You need help," Kos said. It did not sound like an insult, but a genuine statement of concern. "Irelad were not meant to last this long. Your programming is deteriorating."

"That is why I sent you to find Desidario," Ahto shouted. "My time is running out, and I need him to fix me."

"I will gladly help you," Kos said. He waved a hand behind him for Orinthia and Thrutt to come forward. "But you have to let them go. This man is hurt and needs real medical attention."

Orinthia clung to Thrutt's elbow and walked in sync with him.

"Let them pass, and I will stay," Kos bartered.

Orinthia's mod hummed as he spoke.

Ahto turned his arrow-shaped head to look at all of them. Even in the pulsating light, she could see his artificial intelligence working through his options. "You two. Get off my ship," Ahto ordered.

Thrutt did not hesitate. He rushed past the snake toward *Freya* with Orinthia in tow.

Orinthia looked back at Kos. *What are you planning?*

They rushed through *Freya's* open cargo doors. Orinthia let go of Thrutt's arm and stood at the mouth of the sloop watching the two she left behind. She could hear Thrutt jump from the top deck to the lower without using the stairs. The ship rocked when he landed. It was all she could hear. Kos and Ahto were too far away for her to make out what they said. She leaned out her head. *Freya's* engines came to life, drowning out all other sounds.

Her head was in a fog and she could not understand what Kos was playing at. He had lied to Ahto, but why?

"Orinthia, close the doors," Thrutt said over the speaker.

Orinthia looked at the lever. It still had a gash from where Kos had kicked it when he rescued her. How were they supposed to leave him behind? She tried to think of what to do. There had to be something she was missing.

Then she saw it out of the corner of her eye. Her booster pack sat a few feet away from her. Was this his plan? She was not sure, but it was going to be hers. As fast as her worn body could manage, she grabbed the pack, spun around, and tossed it out the open door toward Kos.

The engine masked the sound of the booster smacking the ground. Ahto did not turn around.

Kos threw himself forward, catching the pack with his

hands. He had just enough time to put the straps on before Ahto reacted.

The snake reared up to strike, but as he brought himself down, Kos ignited the jets and rocketed away. He flew across the bay, straight for *Freya's* opening. Orinthia stepped aside and kept her hand on the lever.

Ahto was up again, trailing behind Kos. He was right on Kos' heels.

Orinthia made a split-second choice to pull the lever down and close the doors. The opening narrowed, and she watched with wide eyes as Kos' chances of escaping grew slimmer.

He turned to his side, slid through the inches of room left, and crashed into the wall in the back of the hold. The hatch sealed.

Ahto collided with the outside, making the doors shiver.

"*Freya*, launch!" Kos shouted.

The ground beneath them lurched. Orinthia toppled over. The momentum forced all the air out of her lungs, and it took a moment to refill them.

When they reached velocity, she stood up, using the wall as support.

Kos laid on his back, staring at the ceiling. If he had not spoken a second before, Orinthia would have assumed the impact had knocked him out.

"Are you okay?" she asked in a dry voice.

"Yeah." Kos did not look up or move. "You?"

"No less than usual."

"Good." He took in a deep breath and let out a long sigh, wincing as he did. "I think I'm going to stay here for a minute, if you don't mind."

Orinthia nodded, understanding his meaning, and left the hold to find Thrutt. She gently lowered herself down the ladder, almost slipping before she reached the bottom. There was a dent in the floor from where Thrutt had taken the faster route.

As she moved by the small quarters, she could see Uri on one of the bunks. Her body refused to enter and her feet made her move on to the control room.

Thrutt stood at the helm, punching in something on the screen and flipping switches.

"Where are we headed?" Orinthia asked. She stepped in and stood beside Thrutt. It was the first time she had seen the cockpit from the inside.

A window spanned the room in a half circle. There were three seats, and the space between them was only enough to walk through to get from one side to the other.

"Not sure, yet," he answered. "Kos will have to plot a course. I'm trying to mask our signal to keep us hidden."

"Do you think Ahto will come after us?"

"Eventually, yes."

40

*W*rappers from the food Orinthia stuffed in her mouth sat scattered around the galley table. She ate until her stomach hurt, then polished off two more protein cubes for good measure. The fog she was in lifted enough for her to think through what all had happened.

As she processed the events, the last piece of her water sphere dropped with a splat to the ground. She left everything she took from Earth on the *Fera*; most importantly, the picture of her and her mother. Orinthia's hands shook as the realization set in. It was the only thing left she had of Jean, and it was gone.

"What's the matter?" Kos asked.

Orinthia had forgotten he was sitting across from her and jumped at the sound of his voice. "We left everything," she whispered.

Kos nodded as if to say the same thing had been on his mind.

Another thought hit her as the sadness of her loss settled. "Hey, I never got paid."

Kos chuckled. "Now *that* is unfortunate." He leaned over

and pulled out the cloth pouch from his coat pocket. "The cargo we stole from the EC ship never got sold. But here, it is the quartermaster's duty to make sure the crew is compensated."

Three blue credits dropped in front of her on the table. Orinthia picked them up. Only three hundred credits for nearly dying more times than she could remember. It was not the riches Thrutt had promised.

"This is a mess," she said, putting the credits into the pocket of the sweater she found in one of the bunk's storage containers. Her eyes moved to the galley's exit and she recalled what she had avoided thinking about. "What am I going to do about him?"

Kos looked toward the bunk rooms, then back to Orinthia. "Do you want to talk about it?"

The question lingered between them. Did she want to talk about it? "You're sure he's not dead?" she asked.

"I did a full scan. His central operating system is still intact. It's a chip in his brain that controls the rest of his body. That's where 'he' is. He doesn't have a heart like you and I do. The chip is like a defibrillator for his brain. But the rest of him is severely damaged. Thrutt patched up the tubes, so they should stop leaking long enough to get him somewhere they can do real repairs."

Orinthia shivered. There was only one place cyborgs from all galaxies went to receive care. But the Moon colonies were too close to Earth. Hunters patrolled those sectors regularly, and with everything that had happened, she was sure they would send more ships out. "Is there anything we can do without a hospital?"

Kos shrugged. "I'm not a cyborg expert. Only enough to do basic care."

Orinthia's head fell back and she closed her eyes, trying

to think of any way to get Uri the help he needed. There had to be someone else. The universe was vast.

Thrutt's heavy steps moved down the corridor and stopped inside the galley. "I hate to eavesdrop, but you two talk so loud."

Orinthia rolled her head to rest on her shoulder and opened her eyes.

"There is someone who can help," Thrutt continued. "It makes me sick to consider it, but if you really want to save your brother, I don't think we have many options left."

The instant he said it, Orinthia knew who he meant. Her heart raced and hands went cold. "My father."

Thrutt sat down and put his elbows on the table. "You said he built Uri after his accident. So, he would know how to fix him."

Orinthia wrapped her arms around her chest and looked away from Thrutt. Was this all part of Errol's sick plan? He had told her where to find Desidario.

"We'll be right there," Thrutt said. "I won't let you face him alone."

"Neither will I," Kos said.

The weight of the room folded in over Orinthia. She buried her face in her arms. Tears streamed down her face and dripped onto the borrowed clothes. She spent her life wishing to get away from him, but now she would have to go to him and beg for his help. Her cry turned to choking sobs. The life she wanted to be free from loomed in front of her, daring her to make a move so it could swallow her again.

A scalding hand touched her arm. "I promise he won't hurt you."

Kos's words trickled into her ears and pulled her back from the edge of her despair. She pictured the little boy in her dreams standing between her and Desidario. The Kos Rogue before the military took his offering and molded him into a soldier.

"You two don't owe me anything," Orinthia said between hiccups. "Why are you helping me?"

The table groaned as Thrutt leaned forward and touched her arm, too. His hand cooled the skin beside Kos' hand. "If you haven't noticed, that's what I do."

"And I've done enough damage in my life," Kos said. "I can afford to do some good."

Orinthia looked up, her vision blurred. She blinked until she could see their faces clearly. The grey stone man and his human best friend. Their patchwork family opened and invited her in. She was still broken, but so were they. Neither of them asked her to change to fit their standards. They welcomed her as her, flaws and all.

"Thank you," Orinthia whispered. "Uri and I need the help. And even if it terrifies me, I think I can face my father for him."

Kos straightened and let his hand fall from her arm. "I'll start working on a route. I'm still not convinced Elendoras is real, so we'll have to make some stops before we head there. Ahto is looking for Desidario, too. It's now a race."

"For now, you rest," Thrutt said. "We'll take care of what we can and deal with everything else when we get to it."

Orinthia gave him a weak smile. She became a marauder for adventure and to see new worlds. To meet creatures beyond her imagination. To live one heartbeat at a time. The way it happened may not have been how she had planned, but looking back on her journey, it was exactly what she got.

Get a free bonus short story at TheShortWriter.com

ACKNOWLEDGMENTS

I've been humbled by this experience. The Fera is my first full length novel, this being the second edition. As I'm writing this section, it's been over two years since I wrote the original. My grandma, the last grandparent I had, passed away the day I hit "submit" on Amazon. Since then, my whole life has changed, including a new child and the loss of my father.

My husband has been there for me through it all, including encouraging and pushing me to continue. "You were never more happy than when you wrote," is what he told me. When my time on this planet has come to an end, I hope those words grace my headstone. Thank you, my love, for staying up late as I talked through plot holes, characters, and crazy ideas.

Thank you to Paula for helping me edit the first edition. You were there for me when I was too scared to ask for help. I know you don't like alien books, but you're a blessing for doing it anyway!

Lastly, to my children. I hope you two grow up and follow your dreams. I will be here, cheering you on. Just, don't be like the siblings in my stories, okay? Love each other like Orinthia and Uri. Thank you for sharing your mom with her other (book) children. Someday, when I'm gone, these stories will be left for you. I love you both.

ABOUT THE AUTHOR

Lorena Para (1990-present) was born in Southern California. Her parents moved to The Land of Enchantment (New Mexico, USA) in 1993, where she lived until high school graduation in 2008. She moved back to California and attended college. While working on her bachelor's degree in Elementary Education, she met her husband. They live together in a small mountain town tucked away between Los Angeles and Fresno, along with their two children, dogs, chickens, ducks, and hobby homestead.

Lorena is a fan of writing science fiction, dystopian, and post-apocalyptic genres. She finished her first self-published series in 2020 and is currently working on an expansive space pirate series.

When she isn't writing, she is running a small handmade sticker business, homeschooling, her daughter, playing video games, and consuming all forms of Star Wars media.

Stay up to date by joining her newsletter crew:
https://mailchi.mp/theshortwriter/book-signup

f facebook.com/theshortwriter

⊙ instagram.com/theshortwriter

ⓟ pinterest.com/theshortwriterLP

g goodreads.com/theshortwriter

ALSO BY LORENA PARA

The Lenore Monroe Series

Short Autumn Days

Last Winter Days

Cloudy Spring Days

Wavering Summer Days

Space Marauder Chronicles

The Fera

The Gravity of Elendoras